NOVELTY

NOVELTY

and other stories

Caleb Caudell

BONFIRE
BOOKS

Published by Bonfire Books,
753-755 Nicholson Street
Carlton North, VIC 3054, Australia
info@bonfirebooks.org
www.bonfirebooks.org

ISBN 978-0-6457768-1-2

A catalogue record for this book is available
from the National Library of Australia

"Forbearance" and "Learning to Live" have appeared in different form in *Expat Press*

Cover: *Degustation*, mixed media on paper—Lucas Smith, 2023

Also by Caleb Caudell:

The Neighbor

To Marj and Leslie, my sweet kitties.

CONTENTS

CELIBACY

"WHAT IF I GOT A CAR? We could have some privacy. I know a place we could go."

Aaron looked at Louise like he had to pin her down with his eyes or she would slip away.

"You don't have a job. How you gonna get a car?"

"I'll borrow some money from my old man."

They stood on the sidewalk outside the post office. Louise looked at him with flat and lightless eyes. Her dress billowed in the breeze.

A fat man in a wrinkled suit walked toward them and Aaron stepped onto the road. Louise watched the fat man shuffle by.

Doves called. The day eased into evening and the sun dulled behind clouds that spread through the sky like splotches of water.

"What do you think of that?" Aaron asked.

"I don't know. You think your dad'll give you money for a car?"

"I know he will. I got about half of what I need."

"I don't know. Maybe. I need to go."

He tried to smirk but his lips trembled. White-hot butterflies in his belly, his chemicals coming to a boil.

"You going to see Rodney, aren't you?"

"No"

"Him and that damn car. Just because he works at the bank and has a car. Thinks he can drive up and down these streets like he owns the whole town."

"I don't know what you think I'm out doing but it's not like that."

"Bullshit. You lying whore. Goddamnit what is with your kind? Just because he has a car and I don't. I'm gonna get me a car and then you'll see. Once I do I won't give you the time of day, it'll be too late for you. Just think about that," said Aaron.

She turned away from him and walked. His face burned and he ran after her but then he stopped and watched her disappear into the bleary horizon. After standing with clenched fists for some time he walked farther down the street and went into a diner. Meat sizzled on the griddle and men grumbled at the counter.

"Hey, Aaron. Got a stool right here next to the register. Have a seat."

Dave the owner stood behind the register in a white T-shirt stained with sweat and grease.

"You hungry?"

"Yeah I could go for a burger."

"What's the matter? Your face is all red."

"It's nothing."

Aaron watched cooks press burger patties on the range. Crack open eggs and spread hash browns. The diner buzzed with talk and plates smacking on counters and the dinging bell of orders up.

A burger sat before him. By its side on the plate lay the top bun with two pickles and a ring of onions. A mound of bronzed French fries. When he slid the plate closer a few fries tumbled onto the counter and made a dry sound like rustling twigs.

"Hey, Aaron, whatever it is, don't let it get to you, eh?"

Hoarse laughter.

Aaron nodded and then put the burger together and ate. He stared at the wall. Men in aprons passed in and out of his careless cone of vision and all he felt or knew was the juicy meat in his mouth, the sharpness of the onions and pickles and his throat grabbing and dragging the mash down like a scaleless snake inside him.

Alternating burger and fry, leaning over the plate. Elbows on the counter; the world he saw without seeing and the sounds he heard without listening. When he finished he sat up and leaned back and looked over his kingdom of crumbs. Wiped his face with his forearm and got a few bills out of his wallet and tossed them on the counter.

"Hey Dave, you keep the change."

"We'll see you around."

He passed through the door and stood on the sidewalk and felt the churning food. A car rumbled along. His anger came back as if an imp had dialed in a piercing radio frequency and he thought of Louise. He thought of Rodney and that new car at the curb and her getting in with a look in her eye, a look she would never give him.

Her pupils spreading and shining. Not for him. Never for him. He had no car and no job and what money he had he spent on burgers and fries and now he wanted a soda.

With knotted muscles he walked, onion on his breath. Every now and then someone stepped out of his way.

A few miles down the street he turned left onto gravel where the town met the woods. The sun went under the amber skyline. Gnarled branches blackened in the dusk. The cool air pulsed with hoots and chittering insects. He thought in painful pictures. A hot iron brand in his brain. Louise on her back, put there by passion unknown to him.

Down the gravel until it was dirt. Darkness filling the gaps between the trees. The sounds of restless night.

He saw her teeth in her bottom lip, her hair in the style of rough roving hands. Neck turned up like a sacrifice, her body a tool of someone else's pleasure.

Aaron's knees and feet hurt like he'd taken a beating. Someone else seemed to think within him, a sadistic stranger. He came out of the woods into a field that ended in a ridge overlooking a plain. The night sky curved up and showed halfhearted stars. The moon a faint sliver, the lost claw of a cat.

He saw a car to his left, down a ways. His blood burned and his ears rang. He tottered to the edge of the cliff and looked over the gentle slopes and scattered trees and then he stepped back and lay down in the wet grass.

The dark world throbbed around him. He waited and waited and then he got up and walked toward the car and supposed he would see it moving or hear it squeaking. Readied himself for steamed glass and hands on the pane or the sound of breathing or calls to god or calls to a name not his but nothing happened. He got closer.

The car loomed cold and cryptic. Aaron rubbed his hands on his pants and stood until the sun should've come up or the car should've started but the night stood still with him as if in solidarity with his shame. Then his legs took him farther on and he got up against the back window and he made out flitting shapes and heard low voices. Nocturnal birds called out with urgency as if to warn him away.

He lunged and pounded on the trunk. Before he could bring

his hand back the door opened with a sound like bones breaking and he saw a blur of pink meat moving toward him.

Rodney was naked and panting. A woman's voice called from the car. Aaron tried to kick Rodney in the dick but Rodney batted his leg away and punched Aaron in the face.

"Goddamnit you little asshole, you stay away. If I ever catch you following us again I'll kill you."

Aaron fell, his face stinging and his head swimming. On his back looking up at the sky and wanting it to crush him. The stars to rain down on him like shattered glass. The door shut like a shout and the engine started. Rodney backed up the car and peeled out and slung dirt on Aaron's face.

The car drove off fast, bouncing and swerving with Rodney slapping the side in a gesture of frustration or warning or triumph. Aaron didn't clear the dirt from his face for a long while. He waited for anything and nothing, for coyotes to set themselves upon him or great birds to pick him up and carry him over the ridge and drop him to his death. Tasting blood, he rolled over and pushed himself up.

"I'll get that son of a bitch," he thought.

"He thinks he can just drive around with that new car and do whatever he wants. Just because he has a car and works at the bank and his dad sits on the town council."

Aaron walked down the dirt and gravel path between black leaves hanging like tattered cloth. Bugs roaring like laughter. When he got to town the first threads of light twirled up out of the horizon.

"I could really go for a cream soda," he thought.

A CHAIN OF UNEVENTFUL EVENTS

THE AIR IN THE ROOM WAS STALE. Gus Bunson opened a window. With his back to his girlfriend Margaret he spoke:

"I just want to write."

"Can you make enough to live on it?" she asked.

"I don't know, maybe. Maybe not. Probably not the kind of writing I want to do."

A cardinal landed on the sidewalk and cocked his head and stared at Gus. Margaret stood in the dining room and tapped her finger on the dining table.

"It's fine as a hobby. You know I don't care if you want to write and play music. You need to be practical though. My uncle is hiring. He'll hire you if you go in and talk to him. Just let me help you. You don't have to do it forever. It's a good start. You can do something else if it comes along. You'd probably have to start out in the warehouse, it'd be a lot of boxes. Maybe third shift. You make fourteen an hour, and you can move up. You could work in the HR department or something like that."

He leaned on the sill and watched a cat scamper across the street. The breeze poured in and flipped the pages of an open book on the coffee table.

Gus thought about the jobs he'd worked. Hot greasy kitchens, cold dry stockrooms. The scummy sloshing mopwater. Stinking tasks the working dead carried out to keep the lights on.

"Yeah, I'll call him tomorrow. I really will," he said.

He looked at her hair. A few loose strands swayed like swings on a playground.

"I don't know, I'll figure it out. I'll call him tomorrow. I'm also putting in an application at that café I mentioned. That free jazz pizzeria."

Margaret tapped on the table and looked out the dining room window into the white panel siding of the neighbor's house.

"You've quit the last three restaurant jobs you've had. I don't know if you can be happy with another job like that."

"I'll just do it until something better comes along. Don't worry. I probably won't work there anyway. I haven't shown you yet but I've written some short stories. I think they have potential. But I gotta keep working on them."

The first two years they were together she encouraged him to write. He'd compliment her hair and talk about the wind and streaming sunlight and she'd say he had a way with words. She'd ask him if he'd write her a poem and he'd say sometime.

"You know I'll read whatever you write. I've said you should do it. But we're getting older. Time's moving on. I need to know I can depend on you," she said.

"I know. I don't expect you to do everything for me. I'll get another job, I 'll find something I can stick with. I'll figure it out."

He thought of how fun it was to write, how easy it was to tell a story about average lives. No need for adventure or romance. Wild plots were for those who used art to escape from their lives. He wanted to create art that reminded people of the magic in the mundane.

"I feel like we've had this conversation before and things seem like they'll change and they don't," she said.

Gus stared at Margaret's hand rapping on the table and thought about the story he wanted to write. A loosely bound catalog of moments. Memories and scattered sensations. He wanted to gather and polish overlooked objects and hold them up so people could see them in a new light.

"It's just hard to find anything right now. I've been a little down. I can put in an application at that powerviolence bakery tomorrow morning. I know the assistant manager," Gus said.

He talked while thinking about stories where people drink coffee and fry sausage in a skillet. He could write about old men at a diner, curved backs at the counter. A whole paragraph about the sound of a knife spreading butter on toast. The people in his stories would eat cold cuts and hash browns and smoke cigarettes in the garage on aimless afternoons.

"Gus…"

Margaret had centered herself on both feet. She stopped tapping.

"I think we need to break up."

***

"So, what do you think?"

Ann got up from the chair and went into the kitchen.

"Well?"

"Is that what you think about me?"

"What?"

Water flowed from the faucet.

"You think I'm a nag or something? You think I'm forcing you to live this way?"

Walt Sherwood stood behind the chair and stared into the laptop monitor. Words on the screen blurred in his tired eyes.

"Babe, that story doesn't have anything to do with you. It's supposed to be kind of funny, kind of silly. I'm not saying anything about us," he said.

"Those details are from our life. You just think I'm pushing you into jobs you hate. Is this what you spend all your time writing about?"

"Jesus, no. The guy's supposed to be the stupid one. He's oblivious. He's not sympathetic. It's just a joke about how he's not really paying attention. I didn't mean anything by it. I just wanted you to read something I thought was funny."

Walt closed the laptop and the room went dark except for a funnel of light on the floor from the kitchen. He dug into his pockets and looked at Ann washing a bowl in the sink.

"We can talk about how you're feeling, you don't have to mock me in a story," she said.

"I wasn't mocking you. I wasn't thinking about us at all. Do you really think if I had a problem I'd tell you like this?"

"You mentioned my uncle and the warehouse. We had that conversation last week."

"It was just a stupid detail. It doesn't really matter. I could've used anything. That wasn't the point. The guy was dumb, wrapped up in something trivial that he thought was important. That was the point."

He walked through the kitchen without looking at her and went outside into the damp air and the sweet smell of a new green earth, the smell of a spring night and the sound of croaking bullfrogs in the boggy backyard. He looked into the sky at the dim wasted stars and put a cigarette to his lips.

"Last time I do that."

***

Ashley scooted back in the chair and stood up.

"That's what you think of me?" She asked.

"What? No. It was just a funny story, I thought."

BLINDED BY COLOR

A BLACK GUY LEANS INTO THE BAR. He looks like he's asking for a job. I'm saying he's black because it's relevant to the story I'm telling. If I'm in a room with a bunch of white guys I don't call them white, but if I'm in a room with white and black guys I'd call the white ones white and the black ones black. So you know who I'm talking about.

This black guy has that look about him like he's not here to buy a drink, a real low-class look. When a guy like that walks into a restaurant or a café he's asking for work or he's asking for change. Or a free beer, a coffee, a sandwich, a muffin, whatever he thinks he can get. Black and white guys both do it.

The place I'm in, it's hard to describe. I guess it's a Latin American revolutionary café, without the Latin Americans or the revolutionaries. It's named after some southern jungle country and they painted the building in communist colors. Back in the kitchen it's old white trash.

I can see them from where I'm sitting at the bar. Every restaurant owner in America packs his kitchen with Mexicans and Guatemalans. Restaurants that sort of bring you back to an older white America, places that serve bacon and eggs all day—you go in there and you know who cooked that classic American breakfast? A Colombian.

But this café with a Spanish name and skulls and roses on the menu doesn't even have a brown-skinned busboy. The grizzled old guys back in the kitchen smashing the salsa probably listen to Hank Williams. They probably hang confederate flags from their front porches.

The black guy has a plastic bottle full of red flavored powerade between himself and the bar. He's holding it with both hands, he's pressing it into his belly and he's sticking his head over the counter. He jerks his head side to side; his eyes are shifty. His clothes are dusty. He's wearing a baggy black zip up sweatshirt and loose black jeans. Everything is black and dusty about this guy except the powerade bottle he's holding; that red bottle blazes in the middle of all the black.

I'm thinking, best case scenario this guy is asking for a job, wants to wash dishes or sweep the floors. Sometimes these guys aren't asking for a job, they think they can just hose down a wall for an hour, clean some plates and pick up some change. They don't think ahead; they don't think about holding down a job like a dishwasher or a line cook because that would take a little discipline and some patience. They want to do one thing and get one thing in return and they don't want it to take long.

I'm not just talking about black guys now. All different kinds of guys are like this and they all have big problems. They're dysfunctional and the only work they can do is short-term. This guy, though, he's black and that's worse for him because of how people see him. You see or hear black and your unconscious mind goes uh oh. The news is always talking about it so that's how I know you're doing it. That's how sophisticated the news is these days. They don't just tell you that a black guy was asked to turn down his boombox in the library. They tell you why it happened. They call it implicit bias. It doesn't matter to me one way or the other but I can't help knowing it now.

The scene is starting to look funny to me. I think he's asking for change. The bartender, a white guy, looks a little frustrated but I can't hear him.

I'm saying he's white because he's talking to a black guy, so now your unconscious mind sympathizes with the white one while your conscious mind tries to sympathize with the black one. Then I hear the white bartender say:

"You mean like a shot of tequila?"

And the black guy nods and his head keeps jerking around. Maybe I was wrong about the black guy, but I don't know if he's paying for the shot yet.

The bartender reaches down for a bottle in the rail and that's when I hear a loud bang. My heart pounds like the bass drum at a death metal show and I jump off my stool because I think for sure it's a gun going off.

I know other people think that too because some of them duck, someone yells "shit"; they whip their heads around, a few run out of the bar. The guy next to me, another white guy, a young guy with hair like a samurai, he's twitching like an epilectic. And I admit, after a second or two I look at the black guy. I expect to see a gun and the bartender bent over coughing blood and that bottle of tequila broken on the ground.

The sound that made everyone jump out of their chairs came from the exhaust pipe of a beater that had pulled up to the curb outside the bar. We all realize it was the car and not the black guy and we laugh. If psychologists had scanned our brains with their instruments, they would've said we unconsciously assumed the black guy shot the bartender. At least I'm assuming that's what everyone else assumed too. That's what the news says about this sort of thing. I don't think too hard about it. I finish my empanadas; they're not bad.

BLOOD BASIN

THE DOLLAR GENERAL HAD BEEN DEAD all afternoon. One woman on a red motorized cart bought three cartons of ice cream. One nervous looking man with a face covered in zits came in and walked around and left.

Craig stood behind the counter and spaced out. He was supposed to be sweeping or wiping the counter or dusting the shelves. Scraping crud off the toilets. Restocking the paper towels or filling the soap dispenser.

He didn't wash his hands when he went to the bathroom. Even though the sign in the bathroom said employees must wash their hands. He zipped up and turned on the faucet for a second and waved a hand under the dryer so it would make that blowing sound in case anyone was listening.

He was willing to spend a few seconds pretending to wash his hands, but standing in front of the mirror, having to see his aging reflection, stooping and rubbing his hands together under hot running water, pressing the toggle of the plastic soap dispenser, using the expert recommended technique for the expert recommended length of time, then standing under the dryer and incompletely drying his hands, walking out with moist palms and then touching surfaces teeming with the germs of junkies—it was too much to ask.

The Dollar General was at the end of a commercial strip in a part of town where people fell asleep on their front porch in the early afternoon, where three fourths of the license plates had handicapped symbols, where adult men rode children's bicycles and stood shirtless on the streets and hollered and threatened to beat someone's ass.

Craig rented a room in a boarding house that smelled of cigarette smoke and old clothes and mildew. He ate canned spaghetti and meatballs with a plastic spork he kept in a drawer.

It had been the slowest day he could remember. He bent over and put his head on the counter. Dollar General didn't play music in its stores, unlike every single other place on the planet. Craig felt blood pulsing in his temples. Without music he heard the empty core of existence.

He closed his eyes and dreamed of riding a rollercoaster. Theme parks were his favorite. In the daydream his car clambered up the incline, rising so high he poked through a layer of clouds.

He felt metal tapping the back of his head.

"Hey bitch, open the register and hand over the cash."

Craig raised his head and backed up, opened the register and dumped all the cash and coins on the counter. A stocky man pointed a gun at Craig's chest.

"What else you got back there, bitch?"

"Nothing, that's all the money."

"Give me your wallet, too, bitch."

Craig pulled out his wallet and threw it onto the counter. The man grabbed handfuls of money and stuffed them into his pockets. He opened Craig's wallet and took out a five-dollar bill and two ones and a debit card. Then he bent Craig's license and ripped up the pictures of his ex-girlfriend and dropped them on the floor.

"See ya later, bitch."

The man walked out into the early evening light, whistling, waving his gun, his pants bulging with cash.

Craig drummed his fingers on the table and stared ahead but saw nothing. All objects fused into a wall of fuzz. This was the third time he'd been robbed working at Dollar General.

***

He had the day off. After eating a sticky bun he'd microwaved inside its plastic wrapper, he sat at a table in the damp kitchen and listened to creaking wood, other tenants moving, toilets flushing, the chatter of televisions. He went to his room, opened his closet door and lifted the lid off a shoe box and took out a stack of bills. All his savings.

He folded the money into his pocket, put on his shoes and a light jacket and walked to his car, a rusted Camry. At a pawn shop he bought a 9mm from a short scabby man who laughed after everything anyone said.

After the latest robbery, Craig filed a report and spoke to the store manager and then a regional manager. They couldn't hire armed security or put anyone else on shift with him. The business model of Dollar General was based on keeping expenses as low as possible. Their employees were armed with polo shirts against the desperate violent world. Dollar General had higher profit margins than Wal-mart.

***

Craig couldn't afford to go to a range, so he drove out of town until he came to a field where he could set up soda cans. His aim improved. Can after can went down in the pale green weeds. He drank gallons of soda and he had plenty of free time to practice.

When he got paid again he bought a holster and practiced his draw speed. Some evenings he spent hours pulling his pistol out of the holster. As he watched tv he twirled the gun around and pointed it at characters on the screen.

Days followed days without events, without memory. His schedule changed every week but his life was always the same. Wake up and work. Wake up and watch tv and eat frosted apple turnovers. Walk to the corner store to buy lottery tickets. The first ticket he bought seven years ago he won a hundred dollars. He hadn't won a dollar since.

Some days he worked in the morning. Other days he worked in the evening. Some weeks he worked all weekend. He loved watching westerns and crime dramas and wondered what it was like to kill someone.

On the job he daydreamed or played games on his phone and then he went home and ate canned ravioli and watched westerns and put off doing the laundry. Craig wore the same pair of underwear for at least a week. The only thing that gave him any joy was his handgun.

He brought it with him everywhere. To the corner store when he needed lottery tickets and spaghetti and breakfast desserts. To his brother's house on the other side of town. He had it holstered at his side all day at work.

***

One hour until close. Craig was alone in the store. He could've cleaned the bathrooms but he stared at the shelves and then drew his gun and pointed it at a stuffed giraffe.

"Okay, motherfucker. You messed up bad this time. I've been watching you. I know what you're up to. You think you can prey on the weak?"

The doors slid open and Craig holstered his gun and scratched at the counter.

A hunched woman with wiry hair puttered in toward the counter.

"Excuse me young man, do you have pepto dismal?"

"Aisle three."

When her back was turned he whipped out his gun and pointed it at the giraffe.

"Don't think I've forgotten about you."

The door slid open and Craig holstered his gun. This time a man in a baggy blue sweatshirt and blue sweatpants and a gold-colored chain walked in, stopped, looked around and stared at Craig.

"Can I help you find anything?"

"Naw I'm good."

The man moseyed down the cluttered aisles. Craig spaced out again, tapping the upturned butt of his gun. He imagined himself kicking down a door and lunging into a room with two men standing over another man tied to a chair.

Bang bang bang bang. Craig shot the standing men in the chest. They fell and squirmed and cursed and spit blood. Craig walked over to the man in the chair and tore the duct tape from his mouth.

"Thank god you got here. They were just about to cut my dick off."

"You owe me," Craig said.

"Excuse me, sir."

The woman set a pink bottle on the counter. Craig scanned the bottle and smiled. The man in blue stood behind her, looking from the door to the counter. His hands were in his pockets.

"Find everything you need alright?" Craig asked.

"Oh yes, everything just fine," she said.

"That will be four twenty-five."

"You know, they call this place Dollar General. But most things cost a lot more than a dollar," the woman said.

"Yeah, it's just a catchy title."

The man stared at Craig. The woman paid and got her change and pepto and stepped away from the counter and walked to the door.

"Find everything alright?" Craig asked.

The man in blue stepped forward and put down a pack of lifesaver gummies and watched the woman head to the door. He said nothing until she was out of the building and the sliding doors had shut again.

"Naw, I didn't find everything alright. Why don't you hand over everything you got in that register homeboy."

He pulled a gun out of his pants and pointed it at Craig.

"Hold on just a second."

"Come on, asshole, I don't have all day. Give me the money or I'll blow your head off."

Craig nodded toward the gun at his side.

"I think you should get out of here," Craig said.

The man in blue glanced at Craig's hip.

"What, what are you gonna do? You gonna fucking shoot me?"

"Yeah."

"Fucking cashier's gonna shoot me. Motherfucker if you don't hand over that cash I'm gonna end you right here."

The man in blue looked to the door.

"I don't have time for this shit. Give me the cash or I'm gonna kill you. I shoot motherfuckers for less than this," he said.

Silence. The man's upper right eyelid quivered.

The doors slid open and the man in blue flinched and Craig drew his gun and fired three times, twice into the man's blue belly and once into his throat. The man made a horrible choking sound and blood burst from his windpipe as he fell back into a shelf, knocking down earphones and phone chargers and prepaid phone cards.

Craig held his gun out, as if frozen. The man let out his last bloody breath. The old round man who had walked through the door stood in the entrance with toothless mouth agape, holding his hands up.

The next day Craig sat at a plywood desk in a small airless room. The store manager on the other side of the desk brought his hands together and said:

"I'm sorry, we have to let you go. It's against store policy for an employee to carry a gun."

Craig wasn't charged. Two months later he was still out of work. Killing a man felt like nothing.

NOVELTY

FRANCIS MET MIRANDA on a dating app. When she showed up at the bar she was prettier than her pictures. That had never happened to him. He figured she'd flake, so he brought a notebook and sketched an outline of a philosophical novel he intended to write. Some vague intuitions about the effect of technology on human nature.

Their first date was beers and laughs and talking with their hands, the gestures of silent movie actors. Eye contact that popped like grease in a pan. They ended the night kissing in a deserted parking garage. November air chilly and wet. Glowing lamps. The aura of an underwater dream.

They spent the next five nights together. A month later they agreed to be exclusive. For Miranda this meant making her instagram private, no longer sending sexy pictures to bored married men dabbling in the destruction of their families. She grew disgusted at the thought of touching another man.

But Francis looked at other women like a cat that has heard birds chirping in the bushes. His head cranked out images of what lay beneath tight shirts and jeans. He stared with a slackened jaw at yoga pants fighting a rearguard battle against relentlessly advancing butt cheeks.

He would enjoy a smoldering glance from a cashier or a flirtatious exchange with a coworker, and he would worry about missing out on the carnal variety of life. But he let his relationship envelop him, he endured it like the weather.

After six months of dating, Miranda moved in with Francis. Her dog got the spare bedroom. Francis acted the part of a loyal boyfriend while his soul was on pornographic holiday. Over time they fucked less. He'd say he was tired after a long day at work. But if a new woman had offered to suck his dick at the top of Mount Everest, he would've set off with boundless energy.

Their life crept along, Miranda silently planning their marriage, Francis plotting his escape. On a rainy day after three years together he tried to end the relationship. They both had the day off and they sat in a haze of frustration. The rain on the roof sounded like futility. He talked about the discomfort of being tied down. When he saw her eyes swelling and reddening he said everything would be fine. He needed to work out more, eat better and make new friends.

Two months later they were in the living room on the couch. The sun had set. A dark and realistic sex drama played on tv. He said this isn't working, we should see other people.

This time he held his ground. Miranda cried with the resonance of ancient Greeks lamenting a tragedy. Through her sobs she spoke of all that had been lost. Francis offered to help her move out and find a new place to live.

That night Miranda went to stay with a friend on the other side of the city. The next day Francis rented her a moving truck. A week later most of her things were gone.

He wanted to date. Nothing serious, just a night out here and there. He redownloaded the apps and asked out a woman from work. The date was dull. He told her outside her apartment that he'd had a good time but he was still getting over his last relationship. She said see you soon and never thought of it again.

Now that he was single, women seemed less available. It had only been three years but the apps were a different game. He lost whole evenings to fruitless swiping. Beating off to pictures of women less than a mile away. Simulated women selling porn subscriptions. Bathroom mirror pics, one ass cheek plumped up from half-sitting on their sinks. Women who sent the first message looked like burn victims and elephant seals. They were over forty. The peripheries of their pictures shrouded in black sludge, grainy and ominous like unearthed documentation of a horrendous crime.

Miranda found an apartment and tuned out all romantic overtures. Coworkers and acquaintances feasted upon the news of her single status like rabid jackals in a famine. Men who called her a friend for years said we need to talk, I'm in love with you.

The only man she wanted had rejected her, while every other man in the world drooled and lunged for her like a cretin prematurely released from a mental hospital. Francis denied the one woman who wanted him, while every other woman seemed to treat him like wet shit on the sidewalk.

Miranda worked and took care of her dog. She read large-print books about loving herself and signed up for sculpting classes. Francis worked out six days a week at the gym. He lifted with bad form, on the verge of pulling muscles, yelling at the end of his sets as if he were spearheading a suicidal charge.

Finally he matched with an attractive woman on an app. He

sent the first message. Her name was Kate and she suggested drinks at the bar where he'd met Miranda.

Francis was almost seeing her for the first time when he sat in the booth. She looked like Miranda. But Kate had a bigger nose and her eyes were darker. After they parted with a kiss on a bridge, Francis went home and got in bed and gazed at the shadowed ceiling. Thinking not so much about this one new woman, but about the other women sure to come.

He saw Kate a few days later. They walked in the park, laughing with arms intermingled. The early autumn sun shone with nostalgia for a lost summer. They sat on a bench and watched a couple toss a frisbee to a golden retriever. Listened to birds softly singing. They talked about episodes from their lives.

Afternoon passed into evening. Kate said she was hungry. Francis mentioned a taco and tequila stand a few blocks down the street. They walked quietly triumphant, holding hands, secure in the ever crumbling and rebuilt present. That night they went to Francis's house and fucked without discussion, as if carrying out a wordless destiny.

After a few hours of sleep they woke together in the late morning light. They got out of bed and sat on the porch. A cloudless sky permeated all things with vanity. They looked onto the street at couples walking dogs and the occasional shambling vagrant and they talked about where they might go for breakfast.

***

She came over five or six nights a week. Francis stopped trying to date other women. He kept dreaming about it. One night after dinner, in front of a gritty television crime drama, Francis glanced at Kate and thought her nose seemed smaller. He looked again and again until she asked him what he was doing.

"You look a little different."

"Haven't changed anything," she said.

But after several looks Francis had convinced himself. She looked more like Miranda.

"What?" Kate asked with annoyance.

He said nothing and watched tv.

***

Francis sat on the couch waiting for Kate to come back from the bathroom. It was movie night.

She walked into the living room and asked if Francis wanted to watch *A Weekend in Cairo*, a spy thriller romance. She said it was her favorite movie. Francis throbbed with nausea.

"Hmm, I've seen that one," he said.

A Weekend in Cairo was Miranda's favorite movie. Early in their relationship they had watched it several times. Francis coughed and swallowed hard. His Adam's apple rocketed up his throat and back down again like a piston in a high striker game at a carnival.

"Oh, well, we can watch something else," Kate said.

She wandered through the living room with a pensive air.

"Do you want snacks? Should we run out and get anything?" Francis said.

"I think we're good," Kate said.

She walked into the kitchen and opened the fridge.

"We have goat cheese and crackers," she said.

"Okay. Sounds good. Let's just watch *A Weekend in Cairo*. I don't wanna think too much about it."

He found the movie on a streaming service and hit play and turned off the lamp on the end table.

Kate was engrossed in the movie. She ate the cheese and crackers without taking her eyes off the screen. Francis barely watched.

His body slumped rightward, his mouth hanging open, his arms at his sides and his palms turned up. He didn't have the angelic appearance of innocence in repose, but instead looked like a bloated aristocrat passed out at a banquet, his body stuffed with smoked game birds.

***

After seven months together she brought up marriage. Francis said maybe in a year. Inside he squirmed. He still saw himself with women who served him coffee and passed him on the street. It was natural for him to want different body types, different looks, he thought. A man gets sick of the same woman day after day.

Each day Kate's eyes seemed to lighten until they had Miranda's hazel coloring.

***

On the day Kate had finished moving in, Francis looked through his phone for pictures from the beginning of their relationship.

He found a few from the second month. They were under a mural of a hip-hop bear wearing gold chains. Kate looked the same as Miranda.

He went through older pictures. Six years ago he was with Miranda in front of a fountain. She looked exactly like Kate.

Later that evening, Kate said she wanted a chocolate eclair, a treat Miranda loved. As Francis remembered it, Kate raved about cheesecake. He would surprise her with a slice and her eyes would beam with joy.

"I'll run out and get us some snacks. You want any cheesecake?"

"No, I don't really like cheesecake."

"Hmm, I didn't know that."

***

Late fall. The air was thin and cold and the colors never came. Brown leaves fell like dead bugs. Francis worked longer hours and avoided talk of marriage. Kate seemed unbothered. They watched movies and television shows and went to work and talked about the movies and shows.

Most of the time everyone had seen the show but when they didn't, they pretended and laughed and said oh yeah that was crazy or interesting and they hoped that would be the end of it. Sometimes they would say I've only seen part of it, or it was so long ago I don't remember much about it.

No one wanted to admit they'd never heard of a certain show or actor or director because then someone would mention another show or actor and say oh it's by the guy who did ___ and then they would get irritated if the other person still didn't know who or what they were talking about.

There were so many shows with so many seasons. So many movies and sequels. These tired and overstimulated people watched television like it was a job, their true purpose in life.

Francis got a raise and told himself that at some point he would have to get married and maybe even have kids. There would be less time for watching shows but nothing else would change. One cold dry day Kate came over in a sour mood and spoke of ice cream and other treats. She needed something to cheer her up.

"We could go to the corner mart, pick up some gooshers or those fudge knobs or sugar punches. There's that new pastry shop on forty-fourth, they probably have some nice eclairs."

Kate said she didn't want eclairs but maybe some cheesecake would be nice. Francis noticed Kate's earrings. Small silver triangles. She had never worn them before. He remembered that Miranda had worn earrings just like them.

"Oh, are those earrings new?" he said.

"No, I wear these all the time."

They went to the pastry shop and Kate got cheesecake. All the while Francis felt like half of him had been injected with an anesthetic and the other half injected with adrenaline. He was slow and cold and yet his heart pounded and his face flushed. From what he could tell, Kate sensed nothing. She talked and then perked up when she got her cheesecake, ate loudly and made guttural sounds of gratification.

On the phone at work his voice warbled. He lapsed into improper sales techniques, uttered definitive statements, forgot all his training and experience. His supervisor, a fat man in extra-large slacks and big black orthopedic shoes and flaky reddish folds in the back of his neck, sat Francis down and warned him about his productivity.

Francis apologized and blamed his home life. The supervisor offered to get him an appointment with a therapist. A range of services were recommended. The company cared. The man asked if there was anything else he could do. Francis said he would figure it out and everything would be okay. He would get back to selling driveways, appliance upgrades and bathroom renovations.

Shortly after, Kate had an idea. A fun night out. She went to Francis and asked if he would like to see her favorite band, The Filthy Radiators, an eclectic indie rock group with layered vocals.

Francis couldn't remember Kate ever mentioning The Filthy Radiators, and he told himself he would've remembered because that was Miranda's favorite band.

On the night of the show the weather was cold and windy. Bald trees were bunched in austere and disapproving committees. Francis sat on the couch and looked through his phone.

When Kate finished with her hair and makeup she floated through the hall and into the living room. She said she was ready and they left.

Francis drove through traffic. He gripped the wheel and gritted his teeth. Kate watched videos of funny dogs and glanced up on occasion and asked Francis if he was okay. Of course, he said, everything was okay.

He cursed at someone who cut him off. He stomped on the brake as if he were crushing a cockroach on his kitchen floor. Cars ahead and behind erupted in piercing honks like irate geese funneled through a loudspeaker.

When Francis rolled into the parking lot he saw a line of people stretched around the club. Kate clapped her hands twice and turned to Francis. She smoothed his hair and then they got out of the car and walked across the lot and got in line. They could hear a band warming up.

"I hope they play a few songs from Mister Listerine," Kate said as they entered the club.

Everyone stood close, breathing on each other. They stayed glued to their groups and made flagrantly vacuous conversation so as not to get dragged into uncomfortable interactions with strangers.

The opening band straggled onto the stage with an air of practiced nonchalance. Another indie rock band, a local favorite, with a female lead vocalist who alternated between sassy shouting and tender crooning while skinny men behind her stiffly swayed.

Francis watched Kate nod her head in and out of time. He leaned and yelled into her ear that he needed to use the bathroom. His real aim was finding Miranda.

He looked through the crowd, squeezing between people, pressing up against sweaty bodies. The atmosphere of the club was like an unwashed giant's armpit.

As the band played its last song, Francis set his eyes on a woman that electrified him as no musical performance could. It was Miranda, looking as she did years ago when they were together. He shoved his way to her.

"Miranda!"

She turned to him.

"Huh?"

"Miranda!"

He shouted into her face and she shook her head. Francis shouted once more and the woman waved her hands and shooed him away. Francis stepped back; he yelled sorry while continuing to stare. The woman had turned to the stage as the band played their final chord and the song faded out. Everyone cheered and clapped but Francis.

Then he stepped forward and grabbed her arm.

"Hey it's me, I've been trying to get a…"

Before he could finish his sentence, she ripped her arm back and a man stepped between them.

"Hey, back off," he said.

Francis walked away in a daze and stood next to a stinking trashcan. Roadies moved equipment on and off the stage. His thoughts sputtered like a car struggling to start. He was about to pass out when Kate found him.

"Where did you go? You missed the whole set."

"I've been in the bathroom. Must have been something I ate. Wasn't sitting well," he said.

The Filthy Radiators walked on stage and plugged in and the guitarist strummed a chord that rang louder than a jet plane taking off. The crowd cheered.

***

At the turn of Spring Francis went to a psychiatrist. He was diagnosed with several disorders, given worksheets and manuals and put on experimental medication. At coffee shops and bars women blended into the background. His fantasies had been replaced with cotton and white noise. One day he came home to find Kate standing in the living room, rigid and cold. She spoke with a mechanical tone. It was over. She'd decided after much thought, after talking with her friends and her therapist. Francis had wasted her time. She wanted to feel like a woman again, desired.

The news hit him like a report on distant events. She'd moved in and out like a woman on a long business trip.

Kate was gone, Miranda was gone. What remained of them: a shirt and a pair of sunglasses, a bottle of shampoo, ticket stubs, receipts and a crumpled bag from an afternoon of absent-minded shopping.

He threw it all away, piecemeal, without reverence, as if he were his own foreign housekeeper. His performance at work was unaffected.

THE MONKEY GROVE

BEFORE IT CLOSED ABOUT THREE YEARS AGO, old Paul Holmes used to sit in the diner off Highway 37, just outside his hometown of Williams, telling the same story every day about the one time in his life when he did something brave.

Over pancakes and egg sandwiches, he told anyone kind enough to listen about his boyhood in Williams, about how pretty the town used to be and how much fun he had driving around with his dad and brother.

A little town of five thousand people tucked between green hills and meadows with waxen wildflowers. Golden hayfields combed by the wind. He set the scene and talked about the town square, the clothing shop and the hardware store that smelled of shaved wood. Used to be, he would say, the streets were nice and clean and the houses all new and white. Families would walk through the neighborhoods in the evening and smile and wave when they saw each other.

After Paul described the town, he talked about the Monkey Grove and how he worked there one summer when he was twelve years old. One late spring evening he'd been playing with his older brother Danny in the backyard. Playing often turned into fighting, and Danny would beat up on Paul and call him a coward because Paul would run and cry to their mom. On that evening, Paul ran through the sliding glass door, smashing it to pieces. His dad beat him and his brother with a belt and told them to wash up for supper.

That night the family ate mashed potatoes and pot roast in gloomy silence. They stared at their plates and cleared their throats; they chewed and swallowed their food and gulped down glasses of milk. Their father wiped his mouth and dropped his fork, which clanged against the plate greased with gravy.

"Gonna put you both to work this summer. Give you some structure. Give you something to do with all that time you have to run around breaking my windows and doors that I worked hard to provide. Running amok like that with no purpose. Well, soon as school's out you're both going to work. Danny, I got a buddy that's a groundskeeper at the state park, you're gonna help him mow the grass, keep the pioneer village clean, things of that nature. Paul, you're gonna work with your Uncle Dale at the Monkey Grove. He'll put you at the concession stand I figure."

The boys looked up and nodded and then stared at their plates until their mom finished eating and cleared the table.

***

The Monkey Grove was a tourist attraction, a gift shop and a miniature zoo. They sold snacks and lunch food like bologna sandwiches and corndogs, also T-shirts, toy cars, board games and glassware. They kept wolves, bears, monkeys, goats and llamas in cages. The Monkey Grove was open eight months a year and was listed in travel guides and brochures. Travelers stopped to stretch their legs and eat a tenderloin and check out the monkeys.

Paul worked with two high school kids, Ed and Terry, who wore tight white t-shirts and black jeans. They smoked cigarettes and said words that Paul knew were bad. Ed drove a Chevy Impala and Paul dreamed of going for a ride in it. The high school boys teased Paul and made him clean the outhouse.

Uncle Dale did most of the hard work, but sometimes he let Ed or Terry clean the cages. At the end of October, he shot the animals with tranquilizers and carted them on a trailer into a heated storage building at the end of the property. Dale worked all day except for the hour between noon and one when he ate a big lunch in a shack where he stored a few tools and a hunting rifle.

One day toward the end of summer, Paul played in the woods behind the Grove instead of watching over the concession stand. No one had stopped by in over an hour. Paul carried a stick like a gun; he was hunting communists hiding behind the rocks and trees. They had infiltrated the nation, an advanced wave before the big attack.

Crawling on his belly, he heard a faint voice from the small field between the animal cages and the woods.

"Paul, where'd ya go?"

Paul leaned his head against a rotting log.

"You in the woods? Get outta there."

Paul got up, held onto his stick gun and ran between the trees and over the rocks and logs and into the grassy clearing. Uncle Dale stood squinting near the Llama cages.

"Paul, now I'm not paying you to play in the woods."

"There's commies up in those trees. Someone's gotta get em out. They're all over the woods. I'm gonna kill em."

"You got time to kill reds you got time to clean. I just went by the stand and it could use a good sweeping. Why don't you put down your stick there and go on back to where you're supposed to be."

Paul threw down his stick and walked with Dale to the concession stand.

"Pretty hot in those woods, isn't it? Real humid again," Dale said.

"Yeah but I have to protect our country," said Paul.

"Well, I'm happy to hear you want to defend our country, but I'd like to see a stronger work ethic first. You can't leave a dirty floor to go hunt commies. You gotta get your priorities straight. You leave the fighting to the soldiers."

"I want to be a soldier."

"I figure it'd do you some good. Believe me they'd have you making your bed and cleaning your room before they had you killing commies."

As they passed the cages Dale stopped and looked back.

"Hold on, son."

Dale stared at the door of the monkey cage. It was closed but unlocked.

"Did you see anyone go into that cage?"

"No, I was fighting in the woods."

Dale looked around. He walked up to the door and tapped the lock with his finger. The air hung heavy and still.

"Someone didn't lock the cage. Had to be Ed. That kid doesn't have any sense."

A group of baboons lounged in the center of the cage. One monkey groomed another, picking and eating bugs out of his fur. Dale scanned left and right, squinting and scowling. His face appeared dry and etched with furrows like cracked clay in the sun.

"Did any of the monkeys get out?" Paul asked.

"I don't know. Doesn't look like it. Got lucky this time. This right here is an example of what you do not do. Do not leave this cage unlocked. Pay attention to the task at hand. That's the trouble with you kids today. Always getting carried away with your fantasies. And those older boys, always chasing those girls. You stop paying attention to what's in front of you and you end up with a loose monkey."

"But I didn't do it."

"Same attitude that leads to a dirty floor leads to an unlocked cage, and all sorts of other problems on top of that. I don't know what I'm gonna do with you kids. Well, heck, it's my mistake too. I shouldn'ta given that boy a key."

Dale slid a key from his keyring and locked the door of the cage. Everything was quiet.

"Am I in trouble?"

"No, not yet you're not. Now you stay right here while I check and make sure none of those fellars got out."

Paul kicked the ground with his sneaker. Dale walked by the animal cages and into a patch of grass about fifty yards from the shed. He heard footsteps and twigs snapping to his right. A baboon paced back and forth, growling. Dale stopped and squared up to the angry monkey. The baboon stopped and stared with hateful eyes and bared his long yellow fangs.

"Alright buddy, just calm down. Just take it easy there."

Dale held his hands out and backed up, his palms facing the monkey. One foot behind the other.

"Just take it easy."

Then he turned and sprinted for the shed. The enraged baboon galloped after him, howling for flesh. Back at the cages, Paul heard the screams. Terror gripped his heart. He thought of running to the concession stand or the gift shop to get help, but he knew Ed was off somewhere with a girl. He thought of running to the road and flagging down a car.

The monkey yelled but there was another voice, muffled and pained. Paul shook and started to cry but then he thought of all the times his brother called him a coward, all the times he ran to his mom. This time he bolted toward danger, down the row of animal cages, past the llamas who looked on with concern.

Through the sweat in his eyes Paul saw his uncle Dale on the ground with the baboon over him. The baboon had lodged his fangs into Dale's arm and Dale was punching the baboon in the head with his free arm. Paul ran past them and into the shed. He looked left and right and saw a hoe, a shovel, a saw, and then the rifle in the corner.

Sweat dripped off him but he held back his tears. With slick hands he grabbed the rifle. He had shot pistols and a rifle with his dad before. This gun was bolt-action like the one he had used to shoot cans and squirrels. He checked the chamber and saw that it was empty. On the desk in the center of the shack was a crumpled bag and a stack of papers. Paul ran around to the drawers of the desk and opened them one by one. In the third drawer he found bullets. He picked up two and loaded one into the rifle and dropped the other into his pocket and then ran outside.

The man and the monkey wrestled and spilled blood in the dirt. Paul stopped and shouldered the rifle and aimed for the ape. Just as the baboon lunged for Dale's throat, Paul squeezed the trigger. His ears rang. Through the smoke he saw the monkey on his back a few feet from Dale, writhing and kicking up dust.

Dale groaned and rolled onto his side and picked himself up, pushing off the ground with his intact arm. His other arm looked torn up. Paul held onto the rifle and kept it pointed at the baboon, who'd stopped thrashing. A few long seconds passed and Paul lowered the rifle and looked at Dale.

"Gosh, your arm, he got you good. We should call an ambulance."

Dale looked away; he was shaking. He steadied himself before turning to Paul.

"We will here in a minute. Gotta make sure everything is okay and there aren't any other monkeys out of the cage. I sure woulda been in worse shape if it wasn't for your fine shootin' there. You took a real risk firing that rifle. Guess you didn't have too much choice in the matter."

Dale walked up to the baboon and prodded its chest with his boot.

"Sure is dead, alright. Seems you would make a fine soldier, he said."

"He was going to kill you."

"Yeah, I'd say that's what he intended."

"What are we going to do with him?"

Dale looked at his mangled arm and then around the field and back towards the animal cages. No breeze blew or birds called. Paul and Dale stood in the heat over the body. Ants marched over Dale's boots.

"Well, let's go on ahead and bury him out in the woods. You go on into the shed and bring out the shovel and the tarp. We'll put that monkey on the tarp and haul him to the edge of the woods."

Paul went into the shed and carried out the tarp and shovel. He stretched out the tarp next to the baboon carcass. With his good arm Dale grabbed the monkey by the leg and dragged it onto the tarp.

He leaned and rested his good arm on his knee and breathed out. The world almost went dark but he forced himself up and grabbed the two ends of the tarp and brought them together with one hand and dragged the monkey down the field to the woods. Paul walked behind him with the shovel.

"Well, we'll just bury him here at the edge. No sense stomping through all that brush."

"You want me to dig the hole right here?"

"Yeah, go on ahead. I'd do it but I figure my arm'll come clean off if I try. You wanna get down into that dirt pretty good. Don't want a finger or the tail poking up. Don't want a coyote or a coon to mess with it. Ground is real dry right now but you should be able to do some good digging all the same."

Paul drove the spade into the hard ground. The first strike sent his sweat flying. Dale stood and watched. When Paul saw that Dale was watching, he stopped digging.

"What is it?"

"I feel bad about killing that monkey. Do you feel bad about it?"

"I'm not celebrating it, that's for certain. But you don't need to ask forgiveness. It had to be done, unless you wanted it to be me instead of him."

"It's funny how much they're like us," said Paul.

"In some ways, in some ways. You're probably learning in school about how we came from them."

"Do you think we came from monkeys?"

"We all came from God, is what I believe. I don't know about a monkey becoming a man one day out of the blue. And if we came from them, how come they're still here? I'm not a scientist, I can't say. God made the monkeys just like he made us and I don't believe he intended for us to slaughter them. But you did the right thing. It had to be done."

Paul turned to the baboon and looked at the yellow fangs and the limp tongue. The human fingers curled into a claw and the human eyes open and staring up at the empty sky. The pulpy red meat in his chest where Paul had shot him. For some time man and boy stood silent in the punishing heat.

Finally Dale spoke.

"Well, go on ahead now. You got a job to do."

Paul dug with jerky movements, spilling half of what he unearthed as he lifted the shovel out of the hole.

"Steady yourself, now. You're gonna end up taking twice as long if you don't do the job right. I'm gonna go check on the concession stand and gift shop. See if anyone stopped by in the meantime. I'll be back in a minute. When you're done digging, don't move that monkey, you just wait on me."

Dale turned and walked to the concession stand. Paul couldn't see Dale's face break into a grimace.

Flies had gathered on the baboon. Paul shooed them away with the shovel and went back to digging. He was soaked with sweat and his hands hurt and he wanted to cry but he closed his eyes and tightened his lips. The sound of the shovel slicing into the earth and the buzzing flies hypnotized him.

***

Uncle Dale lost his arm. The bacteria had infected the deep tissues. He ran the monkey grove another five years and then he had back surgery and couldn't get around the property. He sold the business to a younger couple who gave all the animals to the zoo but kept the gift shop and the concession stand. They sold the property to another couple who tore everything down and built a diner. It did well for twenty years.

Paul made it through high school and got a job at the stone quarry one town over, a smaller town across a big river that ran diagonally all the way through the state. He stayed in Williams and got married and had two kids. For as long as he worked, he and his family ate dinner every Saturday night at the diner that used to be the Monkey Grove. The kids wanted to go to McDonalds for happy meals and they whined about having to sit in the old man diner. Paul told them it was a special place and they could go to a McDonald's anywhere.

After his kids went off to college and after he retired, Paul sat at the diner every morning and into the afternoon, drinking coffee and eating eggs and smoking cigarettes. Telling anyone who looked at him about the time he saved the day so long ago in the very spot where everyone was sitting and eating and smoking.

The diner was one of the last businesses in Williams to close. It followed all the shops on the square, the hardware store and the auto plant. Today half the houses in town are boarded up and the streets are littered with styrofoam cups and aluminum beer cans. Paul and his wife moved to a town forty miles north. He goes to the gas station with a little side café down the street from his house and sits for hours in the booths, but he doesn't talk about the Monkey Grove.

THE ETERNAL RETURN

LAST TIME WAS SUPPOSED TO BE THE LAST TIME. But yesterday after work I felt restless. I had no plans. I didn't want to go straight home and sit on my couch and smoke weed and watch tv.

The last ten times were supposed to be the last time. Come to think of it, the first time was supposed to be the last time. That's what I told myself when I finally went through with it. I'd been thinking about doing it for two years. Then that third year I got a little desperate.

I've been picking up hookers for a while now. I didn't go out of my way to get caught up in it. I'd just started a new job at

General Systems but I was paying off debt and my credit was bad so I couldn't afford a nice house. The only place I could rent was this little apartment in a real rough neighborhood. The street was covered in trash and ragged looking people stood around doing nothing. My apartment had this old rusted toilet that barely flushed. After what happened with my last girlfriend I couldn't get any more help from her or anyone else. I was on my own.

A couple weeks after I moved in I realized that the women standing on my street were hookers. They looked terrible. Lots of rashes, sores and boils. At first I thought I'd rather die than let them touch me. But in two years I didn't go on a single date. I downloaded a bunch of dating apps but I just used them to beat off.

After that first hooker left my apartment, I took a long scalding shower and almost cried. I remembered myself as a child and saw my mom looking at me while I played in the yard, and then I thought about the innocence and happiness of my childhood and what my life had become. My mom would've been so disappointed.

I got out of the shower, dried off, got dressed, watched tv and ordered a large supreme pizza from Despotic John's and tried not to think about it. The salami and sauce quelled the heartache. I did get heartburn though.

After that first time I thought I'd never do it again but two weeks later I did. The next morning I woke up with a red bump at the base of my penis. I went and got an STD test and it came back negative and then I was off to the races.

Once a week I got a new hooker. I went driving around the city looking for other spots where they might be out walking. Every now and then I would tell myself that I should stop. It seemed dangerous. It was only a matter of time before I got robbed or arrested or killed.

Years went by and I'd been with so many hookers. Then one day I thought I'd pushed my luck far enough, and that the next time I picked one up, something bad would happen. I went a whole month without picking up a hooker. But yesterday on the drive home I turned left on Parker St and headed for Lincoln Ave where I knew I could find one, and I said to myself that this was really it, the last time, and then it would be out of my system for good.

I couldn't tell from farther out but when she got in my car it was clear she was in bad shape. She had a couple of bald patches. She reeked of alcohol and something else I've never smelled before. Once they get in my car I can't kick them out, I just don't have it in me. We drove around for a minute and then I asked the usual question.

"You know where to go?"

"Yeah I got a place about a mile down the road."

"Here?"

"No"

"Here?"

"No"

"Here?"

"No"

Finally I turned down a side street that reminded me of that street I lived on when I first started picking up hookers. I'm pretty sure there was another hooker walking around and she looked much better than the one I had in my car but I couldn't exchange them.

The road ran on for a long time and got worse and worse and all the houses were broken down and I could see people sleeping on porches. At least I think they were sleeping. She told me to turn down this gravel drive and I drove into an alley behind this big old house with broken windows and an open back door.

"This is it," she said.

I was nervous. Now, I always get nervous, but this time was worse. I thought I was getting set up to be robbed or beaten with construction equipment and left for dead in a port-a-potty.

"You sure it's safe? Is anyone in there?"

"No."

I turned off the car and got out and looked around. Overgrown grass and uneven gravel and then a little farther off a chunky bulldog trotted around but he didn't seem to care about us. I was worried that someone would attack me with a hammer or a hacksaw and I'd end up crammed into a crawlspace. Dead for who knows how long before someone found me.

She went on ahead of me into the house and I saw the door was about to break off the hinge. It was dark inside. The building seemed unfinished. My eyes adjusted to the darkness and I could see that the floor was covered in sawdust. Wood beams were exposed and there was no furniture.

My survival instinct screamed at me to run back to my car and get the hell out of there. But then that other instinct screamed right back and told me to go ahead and get what I came here to get. I don't know if I can explain it but I figure some people know what I'm talking about. You can watch yourself doing something stupid, knowing the whole time that it's stupid, and you can imagine yourself stopping, but you don't, you keep doing the stupid thing.

It's like there's a part of you that wants something bad to happen, or is curious about what it would be like, and even though you have this higher awareness and this potential to change for the better, you'd rather choose what's worse and maybe even ruin your life for a thrill.

The hooker turned a corner and I followed her up a set of creaking stairs. We didn't talk. I feared that when I got to the top an oaf would lunge from the shadows and stab my chest with a pair of needle-nose plyers or bash in my skull with a folding metal chair.

On the second floor the hooker led me into a small room with a window looking out onto the street. I looked at the hooker for a minute and neither one of us said anything and then she sat down on the dusty floor. Not knowing what else to do, I sat down and looked out the window at the deep blue sky which seemed so pure and pretty.

Why can't I be satisfied with the sky, which I could enjoy with no risk of being robbed or beaten or catching a crotch disease? Instead of sitting on this hardwood floor in an abandoned house with this hooker, why am I not in a park watching dogs chase a frisbee, or for God's sake, talking to a normal woman? That's what I thought in that moment, but I still didn't leave.

Instead, I handed her a twenty. The hooker grabbed the bill and stuffed it into her bra. Then she reached into her pocket for a small glass pipe and a lighter. She lit the rock in the pipe and inhaled. She blew the cracksmoke until the whole room was thick with an acrid haze.

She took another hit and blew out more smoke. Then another hit. She reached into her pocket and pulled out another crack rock and jammed it into the pipe. I stretched out my legs, unbuckled my belt, unzipped my fly and took out my penis and waved it around a little. She kept on smoking. I jerked on my penis and stared at her.

After another minute she talked.

"We just need to love each other. We are taught to hate, but we must teach love. Love is love. Love will overcome hate."

I didn't know what to say to that so I kept tugging on my penis.

"We are all one race, one human race. We must love each other and embrace our differences."

I'm always nervous doing this sort of thing, and I was even more nervous about being in this building, but when she started talking about love and one human race I was just trying not to shit my pants. Still, I didn't leave. It's hard enough to change direction once you've made up your mind, but when your penis is out it gets even harder.

"Unity and love will bring peace to the earth forever."

I couldn't believe how much crack she'd smoked and she was

still sucking on the pipe and filling the room with clouds. She reached into her pocket and pulled out another rock. That blue sky seemed like it belonged to another universe, like it shouldn't overlook the wretched happenings of the foul earth. The sky stretched on, unreachable, taunting me with its beauty.

"We have to end hatred and bring everyone together. We must stop dividing people. Everyone deserves love and happiness. Love is love."

By this point my penis was soft and shriveled. I looked away from the window and the blue sky and into the open doorway leading to the stairs. The hallway exuded darkness and doom. My imagination tormented me, and for a second I was sure I saw a hulking man in a hockey mask stomp toward me from out of the dark.

I looked back at the hooker still sitting there staring at the floor and smoking.

"Love will defeat hate, we will join together as one. The earth will be free of violence and war and hatred. There will be no more discrimination and prejudice. We will end racial discrimination. We will all open our hearts to each other and know peace and love forever. We are all one race, we all bleed the same color."

Then I heard heavy steps, or something crashing on the ground floor of the house. I jumped up and put my penis back in my pants.

"Hey, I'm sorry, I have to go. Maybe some other time," I said.

I zipped up and ran through the dank hall and down the stairs. Fear surged through me as I expected a group of leprous speed freaks to assault me with car parts and two-by-fours. Without being able to see much, I ran as fast as I could through the house and found the back door.

It was a miracle I didn't trip and land eyeball first on a rusty nail. I ran through the open door out into the weedy back yard, got in my car, started it up and squealed out of there. Didn't look back. I was sweating and shaking and trying to catch my breath. Calmed myself down by going to a Ricky's drivethru and getting a doubleburger and an extra-large basket of twisty fries. Got home and watched tv until I fell asleep.

I still don't know what happened yesterday. But I can tell you, I'm never doing that again. I put in a request to work overtime, so that should keep me busy.

FATTER

DINNER SERVICE HAD STARTED AT TASTER, a fine dining restaurant. Head chef Jeremy Owens stood in the open kitchen and watched his cooks.

"Have we sent out the saffron Foi De Gras yet? We're falling behind here," he said.

"Yes, chef, it's out. We're ready for the candied orange marmalade bacon twisters."

Jeremy was thirty-seven years old, tall and bloated with bags under his eyes. He had tattoos: the pound sign, a pork chop giving off steam, a death metal band logo and a six pack of beer, among many others.

"How was your night off?" He asked a cook named Eduardo.

"It was pretty good. Watched a few episodes of *Skidmark*. That show's hilarious. You know that girl I was talking about? The hot mom? She came over."

"Oh, yeah? Have a good time?"

"Yeah. She's cool. I think I'm into her," said Eduardo.

"Better be careful. Don't get too into her."

Jeremy was twice divorced. No kids. His last marriage ended with scathing status updates on social media platforms. The local online feminist community tried to blacklist him from the service industry.

Eduardo grabbed golden tongs from the counter and picked up a marmaladed bacon strip and laid it on a small white plate.

"That bacon is really looking beautiful tonight," said Jeremy.

He picked up a strip of bacon and dropped it into his mouth and chewed. With his mouth full he said:

"It's alright. I think we need to dial back the sugar. It's a tad cloying."

Cooks and food runners carried hot plates between burning and sharp surfaces, calling out "door" or "behind" or "to the left."

Three courses had been served. The lights dimmed and the dining room settled into an elegant atmosphere. A server named Mathilda came up to Jeremy as he scrutinized a sauce.

"Chef, we might have a problem."

"What is it?" Jeremy asked.

"One of our guests is worried you've served them gluten. They have an allergy."

"Which table?"

"It's the woman at seven. She says she let us know about her allergy when she made the reservations. Did you read the notes for tonight?"

"Yeah I read them."

Jeremy huffed in a show of frustration:

"I'm getting tired of this shit. All these allergies. People read an article and suddenly their whole diet has to change."

"Hey, this is serious. She might get sick."

"I didn't serve her gluten. I read the notes and modified the recipe. Even though these plates aren't the same when you take out ingredients. Every fucking night I deal with this bullshit," said Jeremy.

He stopped and looked around and then went on:

"Food is art. That's something I always stress. Everyone in my kitchen knows that. What we do is art. It follows an exact design. Guests shouldn't decide what I make. They don't tell me how to cook. You don't go up to Picasso and tell him to use different paint or a different technique. You don't tell Cannibal Corpse to tone down their lyrics or their album covers."

Mathilda walked away and a cook named Brick sidled up to Jeremy.

"There's gluten in pretty much every one of these dishes. You didn't say anything about anyone having an allergy tonight," he said.

"Don't worry about it. I'm fed up with all these fake intolerances. It's just a trend. It's ridiculous. Oh, you can't eat bread? There'd be no society without bread. Just watch, nothing will happen. She'll be fine. It's all in her head."

***

The bacon twisters had gone out. Next was the asparagus soup with garlic and parmesan croutons.

"Is this the one with the gluten free croutons for table seven?" A food runner asked.

"Chef Owens, is that the gluten free soup?"

"Yeah, sure."

The runner took the bowl to the woman at table seven. A waitress came by and gave a lesson on the history of the soup, its cultural significance and its personal meaning to the chef.

The woman with the gluten allergy was named Anastacia. She was dining with her friend Jaime.

"My face is burning up. I think it was something I ate earlier, maybe the amuse bouche," Anastacia said.

"Just breathe through it, it'll be okay. These people are the best, they wouldn't mess this up," Jaime said.

Then she asked:

"What did you think of the bacon? That was very creative, wasn't it?"

"It was delicious. It was so good. I just wish I wasn't having a reaction."

They slurped their soup as waiters dashed around their table. The kitchen hummed; peppers and onions sizzled in skillets. Jeremy stood over the pastry station where a tattooed woman brushed a row of muffins with a pistachio truffle oil.

As diners finished their asparagus soup, another tattooed cook removed a single strip of steak from the sauce and placed it on a white plate. He squirted house made sriracha in a zigzag pattern over the steak. Jeremy looked over the plates and then nodded at the cook.

"The marinade smells amazing. They're going to love this one," he said.

A woman's cry was followed by a thud. Forks, spoons and knives clattered on tables. Drinks were spilled, a wave of gasps rolled through the room. Heads turned to Anastacia, who lay on the ground clutching her stomach.

"She's had gluten!" her friend Jaime screamed.

Waiters and guests gathered around her flopping body.

"Call 911! This is an emergency!"

Jeremy thought about the marinade.

"Come on, it can't be that bad" he finally said to Eduardo.

"It seems pretty bad."

The music had been shut off. Jaime yelled into her phone at the dispatcher. Anastacia, covered in rashes, shuddering and foaming at the mouth, got up and glared at Jeremy.

"You served me gluten. I have Crohn's disease."

Jeremy looked at Anastacia with the lusterless eyes of a dullard.

"Jesus, man," said Eduardo.

"You will pay for this," Anastacia said.

She groaned and shook and her eyes appeared all white. She stared at Jeremy and said the word *fatter*. Then she fell to the floor. Jaime and other guests leaned over her.

"Did you see how she looked at you?" I think she put a curse on you," Eduardo said.

"Heh, I'm already cursed. Lay it on me," said Jeremy.

Paramedics burst through the front doors. They spoke hurried medical jargon and picked up Anastacia and put her on a stretcher and carried her out.

"Alright, let's get back to business. We have a dinner to serve. Michael, get started on the squid fritters. Just a minor delay, let's get back on track," said Jeremy.

The cooks went to work. Jeremy stayed in the kitchen and talked of sauces and temperatures and balancing fats with acids. Unsettled guests scuffled to their seats, torn between wanting to leave and wanting to finish their costly meals.

They sat down, coughed and cleared their throats. Some spoke in a strained whisper barely quieter than a normal talking volume. They said, "can you believe that?" or "I hope she's okay" or "I'm very disappointed in the service here," or they related the event to a similar experience, such as a bee sting at a picnic or a piece of roast beef lodged in a cousin's throat at a family reunion.

Others croaked out commonplaces and acted as if nothing had happened. They said, "I like the colors in here" or "that cocktail we had in the waiting room was delicious" for the second or third time.

***

The next day the crew gathered for a pre-shift meeting. Jeremy talked about the new policy: no ingredient substitutions.

"Everyone will know the score soon. I'm going to change the website and our social media accounts. It was too wishy washy before. That's over now. No exceptions. You sign up for dinner, you get what we prepare exactly as we intend to prepare it, down to the last speck of seasoning. If you have a problem with nuts, dairy, meat, gluten, eggs or whatever, then this is not for you. Plenty of other places will work with you, but I don't need the hassle. Are we all in agreement?"

Heads nodded and yesses and mhmms were uttered in a downwardly inflected tone that sounded like someone stepping on a bag full of air.

"Alright, we've got a ton of work to do today. Lots of garlic to crush. We gotta prep the sauce for the pork shoulder. Our bakers have a long road ahead of them. Those passionfruit cups are going to take some time. I want everyone moving fast and keeping their spaces clean."

The cooks headed to their stations. Jeremy's stomach growled. He lurched into the kitchen and made himself a steak sandwich and ate in a rush, chewing with his mouth open. When he finished his cheeks glistened with aioli.

"Chef Owens, I have a question about how we're doing the tartare tonight," said a cook.

"Hold on, I'll be over there in a minute. Just batch out the mustard for now."

"Uh, Chef Owens, I think we're going to run out of caviar chevre," said Eduardo.

"No, that's impossible. We have plenty, check the other fridge, I think it got moved. If someone didn't prep enough, it'll be their ass."

***

Another night of service. Jeremy walked through the kitchen and looked over shoulders and criticized cutting techniques. His stomach rumbled and he felt faint.

He stopped behind Eduardo and watched him batch the pickled carrots. Eduardo felt a heavy presence behind him.

"Everything okay, chef?"

"Maybe. Just checking on those carrots. I need them to be crisp. Need that brine to be perfect," said Jeremy.

"We followed the recipe exactly. We've been working on getting it right for weeks. I think this is the best batch yet," said Eduardo.

Jeremy stood with a vacant look on his face and then he grabbed a couple of carrots and chomped down on them, his lips smacking loudly.

"Damn. I'll give you guys some credit on this one. The coriander is coming through, but it's not overpowering. Better than the last batch for sure. It's close to perfect."

He grabbed a handful of carrots and shoved them in his mouth. He took more from a cutting board laying nearby. After eating the big batch and running his tongue over his mouth he spoke:

"Almost. Almost there. Maybe adjust the turmeric. Just dial it back a little."

"Yes, chef."

Eduardo turned back to his counter and finished sorting what was left of the carrots. The first guests were sitting down at the counter in front of the kitchen. The men wore baggy collared shirts and slacks. The women wore dark dresses and gold and silver jewelry. They gave Jeremy and Eduardo perfunctory smiles, their lips tight over their teeth.

"I need to review some paperwork. I'll be back in a minute. Once you're finished with the carrots I need you to prep the watermelon salad," said Jeremy.

Brick came by and spoke to Eduardo.

"Chef seems a little off tonight."

"I don't know, he's probably just a little stressed," said Eduardo.

"He ate half the carrots. Are we even gonna have enough for service?"

"He was just tasting them."

"Some of the guests gave him a weird look when they saw him chowing down."

"I wouldn't worry about it. He's under a lot of pressure," said Eduardo.

There was a pause and then Eduardo went on:

"I trust him. The dude's a genius. We're lucky to work for him. He's the best in the city."

"I think the stress is really getting to him," said Brick.

In the employee bathroom, Jeremy sat on the open toilet, legs splayed, pants up, munching on a sloppy joe sandwich. Saucy meat slipped from the bread and plopped into the water.

***

It was a bright and beautiful day. Early fall, the first flush of color in the leaves. A blue sky with fat white clouds languidly passing. Seagulls cried and swooped down on the water shining in the sun. Jeremy walked along the pier, his hands in his pockets, his breath heavy.

The boards creaked under his feet. His belly grumbled. It was lunchtime. For breakfast he'd eaten three dutch baby pancakes and two tubes of sausage. His mind was fogged. He needed to think up new dishes for the fall tasting menu. A reporter for *Gorge* magazine would interview him tomorrow.

When he felt distracted and restless he walked. Went to the lakeside district and popped in and out of the shops. Left his phone at home and let his mind wander, hoping he would happen upon a brilliant dish the same way a mathematical genius discovers a world-changing formula in the shower or while sitting under a tree, staring off into space.

But nothing came today. In a daze he walked away from the lake and got to a row of stores along the boardwalk. An ice cream shop appeared to his left, radiant in the sun, its glass storefront lit with heavenly light.

Bells jingled when he shoved open the door. Three people stood in front of him. One older woman in a shabby coat and messy grey hair walked back and forth and pointed at tubs of flavored ice cream.

Jeremy waited and ran his tongue along his teeth. After what felt like hours he stood before the ice cream.

"Hows' it going?"

"It's going fine. How are you today?" asked the man with sagging skin and tired eyes behind the counter.

"I'm good. Can I get three scoops of the butterscotch and english toffee?"

"Coming right up"

Jeremy watched the man bend over stiffly and scoop the ice cream into a paper bowl. The man sighed and then stood up and handed over the ice cream and walked to the register.

"Okay, that will be seven-fifty."

Jeremy gave the man his card and before he got it back he grabbed a plastic spoon from a cup and took three huge bites. He signed his check and walked to the door.

"Have a good day," said the man.

A young couple entered the shop and stared at Jeremy. He was panting and had ice cream all over his face. They stood together and then parted and walked around him as he ate. Soon his spoon scraped the bottom of the bowl and without thinking he turned and got behind the couple.

***

The last dish of the night had been served. Gold truffle torte. It was midnight. After dessert the guests would have coffee. The restaurant offered cappuccinos and lattes, caffeinated or decaf.

The cooks were tired. They cleaned their stations and talked about the night, talked about each other; who messed up what, who did what well. They talked about the shows they'd watched and the shows they wanted to watch.

No one had seen Jeremy in an hour. Sometimes he went out back to smoke weed, lean against the wall and lose himself in thought. When he wasn't thinking about food he thought about his ex-wives and his guitar. He hardly played anymore. He didn't date either. Every now and then he'd take a woman home that he'd met at the restaurant.

Tonight he was in one of the stockrooms. He found himself there, snapping into reality as if he'd come out of a coma. His hand was in an open sack of flour. The light was off and he could barely make out the cans and bags on the shelves.

His stomach churned. After yanking his hand out of the flour and smacking it on his pants and leaving a ghostly print, he went to a shelf and grabbed a can of tomato sauce. He walked to a desk and opened a drawer and pulled out a can opener.

The silence and musty smell of the stockroom suffocated him. Jeremy looked around and sweated and opened the can and chugged the sauce. The can clattered to the ground and he gasped for air.

With a ring of sauce still around his mouth, he staggered into the kitchen and belched.

"Sorry, guys. Got held up with some order sheets."

***

Middle of service. Main course, glazed octopus. Black-clad food runners and servers carried plates up their arms; they cut through the air with grace, deftly avoiding each other and tables and arms and legs of guests.

The room was loud with chatter. Silverware scraping plates, cups clinking. Electronic instrumentals, hip hop backing tracks. Guests took pictures of their food, their drinks, themselves.

Jeremy emerged from his office, his eyes clouded and red and his apron stained with glaze.

"Has all the octopus gone out yet?"

"Chef, we might have a little problem," said Eduardo.

Jeremy licked his lips and held a fist to his mouth, stifling a burp.

"What is it?"

"We're lower than we thought on the red pepper glaze. I don't know what happened. Three tables still haven't gotten their octopus yet and I'm not sure if we're gonna have enough."

"What the fuck? How did you not prep enough?" said Jeremy.

He waddled to the bin of octopus glaze and rubbed his cheeks.

"Whatever. It'll be fine. We'll go a little light on the last couple of servings. They won't know the difference. They'll be wowed by the veal sweatbreads coming up next anyway. Just don't let it happen again," Jeremy said, his apron glistening in the overhead lights.

Eduardo gave Jeremy a critical look and then went to glaze the last octopus plates. Jeremy saw his reflection in the oval glass window on the door separating the open kitchen from the prep area. His face was huge. His cheeks were bulging and inflamed. What he saw was unrecognizable.

He looked down at himself and his belly stuck out over his feet and groin.

"When did this happen?" He asked himself.

He'd put on eighty pounds in a week. He'd always been a big guy, but he'd worn his weight well. Now he looked chunky and misshapen, like a bag of fertilizer beaten with a baseball bat. His shirts had always been baggy but now they looked like crop tops. His jeans were always loose but now they fit like skinny jeans.

He grabbed his sides and shook the saddles of flesh. Felt his way down his legs and looked around. No one watched him. All the cooks and bakers focused on preparing the award-winning food. He looked out on the diners, chewing and talking and laughing, staring at their phones, showing their phones to each other.

Hunger coursed through him. He'd eaten nonstop all day but his belly was a void. He'd sat on the toilet five times. His butthole was sore. He didn't even *feel* fatter. No one had brought it up. He tried to remember if anyone had given him strange looks or insinuated anything about his weight gain.

All he could think about was roasted pheasant and garlic butter. He imagined himself in a field. Above him the birds soared in the sky in cooked form, bronzed and beautiful and seasoned, dripping butter on his outstretched tongue.

Food had become an all-consuming fantasy. Sauce and frosting. Fried cheese and olive oil. The crunch of the crust giving way to a gooey center. Hot thick chili, spiced beef and beans. Cold sodas and beers and rich milkshakes. Everything he'd eaten made him want more. Each bite inflamed his appetite.

He stood in the kitchen, rocked by his cravings. Cooks moved around him, carrying hot trays and skillets and sharp knives. They cracked inane inside jokes and did voices of their favorite characters from their favorite shows. Jeremy watched Eduardo finish the last octopus plates. His brown skin had a savory sheen. Jeremy licked his lips. He pictured Eduardo on a rotisserie.

"He's too thin, not enough meat" Jeremy found himself thinking.

He glanced around and noticed another cook who had a beefy midsection and pendulous tits.

"He'd probably be better brined," he thought.

***

Metallic light from the tv shone on Jeremy's face. He sat in the middle of his couch, deep in the cushion with his ass nearly touching the floor. A crushed box of cocoa puffs lay nearby. It was seven in the morning and he had been awake for hours, watching a show about little people in rehab.

Jeremy turned off the tv and pushed himself up, leaving the couch covered in crumbs and cocoa dust. He took out his phone and looked up the record of guests at his restaurant and called Anastacia.

"Hello?"

"Anastacia? You ate at my restaurant a few months ago."

"What? Who is this?"

"I'm chef Jeremy Owens. You ate at Taster and got sick. We served you gluten. You had a reaction, I don't know, might have been psychosomatic. They took you to a hospital."

"Yes, I almost died. They had to remove a piece of my intestines," said Anastacia.

"Sorry to hear that...I have a question," said Jeremy.

"Yes?"

"Did you put a curse on me?"

"What are you talking about?"

"Ever since that night, I've been eating constantly and getting fatter. I can't stop myself. I wake up in the morning and before I can even open my eyes and reach for my phone, I've got a piece of pie in my hands," said Jeremy.

"Maybe your metabolism is slowing down. Our bodies change as we age," said Anastacia.

"This isn't aging. This isn't my metabolism. That night at the restaurant, you said something to me. I don't remember it exactly, but you cast a spell on me or something," said Jeremy.

"Well, I do believe that our minds have an incredible power to shape reality. We can manifest our dreams through the practice of visualization. We are what we think of ourselves," said Anastacia.

"So you're manifesting me getting fat," said Jeremy.

"I also believe in the cosmic law of Karma. Maybe it is the universe punishing you," said Anastacia.

"Punishing me? For what?"

"For being selfish and arrogant. I don't know your whole life. You'd know better than I would. You might be projecting a lot of negative energy," said Anastacia.

"Cut the bullshit. Whatever it is you're doing, stop it. Stop thinking about it and manifesting it or whatever. I won't be able to leave my house soon. I won't be able to fit through the fucking door," said Jeremy.

He hung up. Seconds later he was inhaling a bag of sour gummy worms like a horse chewing to the bottom of a feedbag. His cat Charlie sauntered by and meowed. Jeremy fixed his eyes on the cat and then looked at his oven. His hungry eyes went back and forth between the hefty cat and his knife collection hanging on the wall.

A bit later Jeremy sat at his counter, hunched over a plate of crispy thighs. The apartment was silent and dark except for the glow of his phone and the sound of his smacking lips. He was eating chicken and reading a review of his restaurant. Charlie slept between his legs.

The review read: "This place has really gone downhill. The last time I dined here, the service was excellent and the food was unbelievable. The pairings were sublime and the flavors and dishes kept me guessing. They used herbs from local gardens and vegetables from local farms. You could taste the native minerals, the surroundings, the terroire, as the french would put it. I thought the chef was so creative.

"After our first experience, my partner and I were looking forward to another enchanting evening after we managed to snag reservations two months in advance. We thought the wait would be worth it. We got into the courses and that's when our evening went downhill. Peaches and cottage cheese? What was the chef thinking?

"It was one disappointing dish after the next. Fried catfish, tenderloin sliders? I swear they were using Hunt's ketchup. Plus, we could see the chef eating constantly with his mouth open. He was spilling sauce and crumbs on the counters.

"By the time we got to the dessert, we just wanted to go home and forget about the whole evening. For as much as we spent, we couldn't believe what we were eating. I want to say that the initial success of Taster went to the chef's head, but it looks like it went to the rest of him as well. We'll never go back, and we advise everyone to stay away until they figure things out. "

Jeremy slammed his fist on the table.

"That fussy prick. What the hell does he know about running a restaurant? I'm under a lot of stress here."

Then he rubbed his tongue against his front teeth and felt a sliver of plastic. He pulled out a piece of the gummy worm wrapper from his teeth and threw it like he was pitching a baseball.

***

Jeremy woke up gasping, his body covered in sweat. He writhed and coughed and felt life leaving him. The room was suffused with a powdery white light.

"God, I can't breathe," he said.

He grabbed his phone from the pillow next to him. It was 3:37 AM. His apnea had been getting worse.

"I can't die yet. Not like this."

He ran his hand through his hair and touched something sticky. The back of his hair was clumped together. An empty bottle of maple syrup lay on the floor beyond his bed.

He texted Anastacia and asked if she would meet him for coffee. Twenty minutes passed. He wanted to read and distract himself from his hunger.

For the next three hours he lay in bed, breathing out of his mouth, his jaw slack, scrolling through pictures of food and videos of tattooed chefs flipping fajitas in skillets. High-definition images of mouthwatering meals. His heart pounded and his breath quickened.

Account after account of new restaurants opening, of hot shot chefs and their weekend food trucks and farmer's market booths. A pop-tart pop up in a pop-art exhibition; hole in the wall hoagies; a fine dining take on fast food; fifty dollar burgers; waiters with masters degrees wearing paper hats. Blazing southwest sauce. Pickled cactus.

Later Anastacia texted Jeremy. She was unavailable today but could meet him the next morning.

In the still dark dawn Jeremy lay on crumpled blankets, his belly bulging. He thought of his first ex-wife and then his second. Both openly declared they hated him and would never talk to him again.

It had gotten harder to remember what went wrong. The fights had faded but what stood out in scenes with vivid colors were the promises, the moments of hope. They'd talked about the kids they were going to have, their names. Where they might move, trips they might take. Restaurants they'd open together.

He rolled off the bed and got up, groaning like a ship tossed about by raging waves. His Taylor acoustic guitar stood in the corner of his room. Shows he'd played flashed in his mind. Teens gleefully punching and kicking each other to his brutal riffs. In those days he didn't care about food. He ate at chain restaurants and fast casual diners.

To support himself while playing guitar he worked in warehouses. Then he got a job in a scratch kitchen. Apprenticed under one of the most talented chefs in the city. Learned how to caramelize, braise, saute and seer with the same delicate artistry he applied to his music.

His heart full of wistful memories, Jeremy picked up his guitar and sat down on his bed and strummed. His fattened fingers struggled to form the shapes of chords. The guitar was out of tune. He launched himself up and gripped the guitar by the neck and swung it overhead as if to smash it against the ground but he felt a stabbing pain in his chest and stopped himself.

The guitar fell and rang with dissonance in the dank room. Jeremy teetered and sat down on the bed and grabbed the sheets and breathed slowly. The pain in his chest subsided.

"I'm going to die," he said.

***

Brick brought the stockpot of fried mac and cheese to Jeremy. The dining room was half full. Bad reviews had driven people away.

"Mmm, smells perfect. Excellent work," Jeremy said.

"Thanks."

Jeremy peered into the pot.

"Did you add the fried shallot shavings?"

"I forgot. Sorry, I can get started on that real fast," said Brick.

"Get started? Are you kidding me? We're serving it in four and a half minutes. We don't have time for that."

Jeremy took off his apple watch which left a dark red ring around his wrist and he rubbed his jowls and looked around as if everyone else in the room shared his outrage.

"I can probably get it done in ten minutes," said Brick.

"What've you been doing? I gave you all fucking day to finish those shallots," said Jeremy.

"I had a lot to do. I've been working nonstop since eleven. I cut and fried all the bologna chips, made the spam salad mix and the new marmalade marinade. I pickled the potatoes and prepped all the chickens. I even helped Jess make the creme filling for the pies," said Brick.

"It's a time management issue. You're not managing your time effectively. You can get all that done in an afternoon if you're not jacking around," said Jeremy.

"I'm doing the work of three cooks right now. You didn't ask me to do this much before because it couldn't be done," said Brick.

Over the last two weeks, Jeremy had fired one cook and two more had quit. Instead of hiring replacements, he piled more work on himself and his staff.

"Don't tell me what can and can't be done. I run this restaurant. I'm working eighty-hour weeks and you don't hear me complaining about it," said Jeremy.

"Dude, the shallots didn't even come in until four this afternoon," said Brick.

"Really? You really want to argue about when the shallots came in? They came in at noon. I'll go get the order form if you want."

"Come on. We can serve the dish without the shallots if you're that worried about the timing."

"We can? Is that why I stay up until two in the morning designing the dishes, so we can leave out ingredients? Is that why I've won the Phil P. Philmore Silver spoon award two years in a row? Because we do whatever we want in the kitchen and ignore the recipe?"

Eduardo slid between them and spoke out of the side of his mouth.

"Hey guys, let's chill out a little. It's getting a little heated. Guests are starting to notice."

"I'm cool. I'm cool. I'd be even cooler if I had cooks that did what I asked them to do," Jeremy said.

"You know what? Go fuck yourself," Brick said.

He untied his apron, threw it to the ground and walked away.

"No, you go fuck yourself," Jeremy shouted.

A few diners stared; others looked furtively.

"Eduardo, get to work on those shallots."

"Uhh, I'm in the middle of the crunch bombs."

"That can wait a minute. The mac and cheese is going out next."

"Okay chef."

Jeremy clapped his hands and it sounded as if two wet hams slammed into each other and he spoke:

"I don't need a bunch of sorry ass cooks. I need dedicated cooks. We're going to find out how much we care about this job. I ask a lot of my people but I always ask more of myself. No one works harder than I do."

"Yes, chef," a few of the cooks mumbled.

Jeremy waddled through the kitchen into his office. He sat down in the rolling office chair.

"I don't need these lazy assholes."

He reached down and opened the bottom shelf of his desk and pulled out a lamb neck burrito wrapped in foil. He took three huge bites and chewed like a wild animal and ate some of the foil and crumpled up the rest and tossed it behind him. With food still in his mouth he opened the bottom shelf on the other side of his desk and pulled out a bong.

He grabbed a lighter on his desk, held the flame over the bowl, inhaled and drew up a column of smoke through the glass tube. The door of his office was wide open. He torched the bowl and inhaled and held his mouth shut and blew smoke out of his nose for nearly a minute.

Jeremy walked into the kitchen. He smelled of skunk and burnt popcorn and his eyes looked like tomato soup with a speck of pepper.

"Did you get the shallots done?" Jeremy asked Eduardo.

"Yeah but I cut myself. I need a band-aid."

***

Every table was taken at the coffee shop. A barista with a sweaty brow carried a black bus tub overflowing with milk-crusted cups and soggy muffin chunks and soaked napkins stuffed into Gibraltar glasses. Jeremy stood in the doorway, blocking the people behind him.

"Shit, this place is always busy," he said.

Two girls in their early twenties stood behind Jeremy, almost saying excuse me, looking at each other and waiting for him to move. Finally he shuffled forward and took a spot in line. Anastacia had asked him to meet at Beseecher, a coffee bar that served floral lattes and inventive cocktails in a repurposed industrial space decorated with plants and neon green signs.

When Jeremy got to the counter he ordered two 16oz malted milkshake lattes. He turned around and thought he saw Anastacia come in through the front. She stood there looking around and he waddled up to her.

"Hey, Anastacia?"

"Yeah, you're chef Jeremy Owens?"

"Yeah, I know I look a little different from the last time you saw me," said Jeremy.

"Oh, okay."

"I've gained a hundred and fifty pounds," said Jeremy.

"Oh, that's not necessarily a bad thing. I don't see much of a difference. Well, let me order a drink and we'll find somewhere to sit."

People kept coming in but no one left. They bunched up by the door, near the register, around the tables. Jeremy saw people unzipping backpacks, bags and cases. They took out computers, laptops, notebooks, phones, tablets, ipads, stencils, paint brushes, canvases, compasses, medical textbooks, posters, index cards. Two women breastfed their babies. One wiry man conspicuously read a Thomas Pynchon novel.

An indeterminately aged barista with unevenly shaved hair put Jeremy's lattes on the bar. Jeremy grabbed one and gulped it down without taking a breath.

Anastacia got a mug of coffee with almond milk.

"Well, I'm not sure when a table will open up," Jeremy said.

"Hmm. Let me think about it."

She closed her eyes. A moment later two medical students in scrubs at a corner table got up and zipped all their books, folders, papers, pens and phones into their backpacks and purses and left the shop. Anastacia glided to the table and set her drink down and waited for Jeremy to squeeze through the aisles.

They sat down and neither of them said anything for a few seconds.

"So, did you just use your magic?" Jeremy asked.

"I don't like the term magic. It triggers negative associations. But I did concentrate on getting a table and I visualized us sitting here," said Anastacia.

"So you really think that's how the universe works?"

"I believe we can make reality match our dreams, through our intentions and imagination. The cosmos is conscious. It hears us, it gives us back what we put into it."

"Sounds like bullshit to me," said Jeremy.

"Isn't that how you live? You had a dream of becoming a famous chef. Then you became one," said Anastacia.

"Becoming a chef wasn't my dream. I wanted to play guitar. I worked hard every day to achieve my dream and it meant nothing. I visualized it every day. All day long I pictured it. Imagined myself on stadium stages playing to huge crowds and it never happened. Now I bust my ass for something I never wanted. Sixty-hour weeks. For years."

"But maybe this is what you were meant to do, even if you thought otherwise," said Anastacia.

"Who gives a shit. Are you going to stop making me gain weight?"

"I'm not intending that. The universe is ruled by the law of Karma. If you want things to change, you need to introduce some positive energy into the world. You could begin by apologizing to me."

Anastacia spoke softly, her eyes glistened. Jeremy chugged the second latte and wiped his mouth.

"This shit never mattered before. Who cares what my attitude is, whether I'm a nice guy or not. I've never needed to care about any of that. All that matters is being good at something. I made myself into a world class chef. I don't need to apologize," said Jeremy.

"It's not about other people forgiving you. It's for your own wellbeing," said Anastacia.

"I want you to knock off the witchcraft," Jeremy said, his eyes wandering to a banana walnut muffin at the next table. He continued:

"I don't have anything else anymore. My fingers are too fat to play my guitar. My mind feels like lard. I can't even think up dishes. Food is all I have and it's killing me."

"I'm telling you what you need to do," said Anastacia.

"Fine, so I apologize and the curse will be lifted?"

"It's not a curse. If you apologize, it's the start of your journey toward a better self."

"Look, if I say I'm sorry, will I get thinner or not?"

"I can't say that. All I can say is, I think you can change your Karma."

"I don't want it to be this drawn-out thing. I need to get better fast."

"I can't tell you how long it will take."

"Ah, for fuck's sake. Okay, I'm sorry I served you gluten. I should have taken your intolerance seriously. I messed up, okay. I messed up."

Anastacia leaned forward, wrapped her hands around her mug and smiled.

***

Jeremy left the coffee shop as fast as he could without saying goodbye to Anastacia. The sky burned bright. Wind shook the trees and knocked red leaves to the ground. He stopped and caught his breath in the parking lot and went on and got into his truck, the shocks squeaking as he sat. Wrappers and bags crinkled around him.

His phone flashed with notifications. New restaurant reviews. He put the phone in the glovebox and started the truck and zoomed out of the lot. Signs for fast food flew past. Donut shops and ice cream parlors and candy stores. Cartoon pigs and chickens and cows pleading to be eaten.

He felt stuffed and sick. Yesterday he'd been unable to drive a mile without pulling into a drive-thru. Down the road he saw a gym and stomped on the breaks and turned into the lot and retched.

The gym was almost empty. No one was at the front desk. Still in his boots and jeans and sweatshirt he got on a treadmill and walked.

FORBEARANCE

THROUGH THE SMOKE HE SAW HIS FATHER raising the ax and swinging it down on to the wood. As if in a dream or seen at a much greater distance, vaporous, as if the old man with his stiff bearing and hard face were himself made of smoke. Above him the sun was setting and a rind of orange light separated the treetops from the darkening sky.

Jarrett sat and stared and his thoughts went in and out of him like breath. His father worked beyond the hissing embers and waving flame of the fire he'd built.

He just has to keep going, Jarrett thought. Enough wood to build a new house and he keeps chopping. The man can't admit he's old. He doesn't have to prove himself anymore.

Someday soon he's going to fall over dead. It'll be in the middle of some such thing as this, doing more than anyone needed or asked for. He already chopped plenty of wood. No one asked him to build the fire. He's just going to chop and chop as if in denial of his old bones.

Jarrett's brother Reed sat to his right. Slumped in the chair, his legs spread out, his feet against the fire. Each dwelt in solitude, one seething, the other vacuous.

Reed straightened and looked at his father and then at his brother.

"He's gonna go all night isn't he?"

"Just try and tell him that's enough," said Jarrett.

"Got more sense than to bother with that."

Jarrett cleared his throat and got up and scooted the chair back. He sat down, his face carved with contempt.

"I don't know how you sit so close," he said.

"I think it feels good. Getting cold out tonight."

"It's not so cold with half your body in that damn fire."

Reed got out a cigarette and puffed and lost himself in the crackling embers and the smell of burning hickory. Sweat gathered about his pits and hairline. The smoke from his cigarette drifted lazily and merged with smoke from the fire.

Insects sang as the sky lost its light. The orange sunset drained and the fire burned hotter and brighter; the flames blazed up in streams, shimmering like an illusion.

"Did'ya ever hear from the drugstore?" Jarrett asked.

"Nah, I haven't heard anything yet."

"You oughta go in there tomorrow and ask em again. They'll give you that job if you bother em enough about it."

"I don't know. Maybe I'll stop by tomorrow. We're doing okay with everyone living here."

"You don't wanna go too long without work. You won't be able to go back."

"Yeah, well, if you work too hard you won't be able to stop," Reed said.

Reed threw his cigarette into the fire and looked about and got up.

"Where'd Aaron go?" he asked.

"He's been inside the whole time," said Jarrett.

"Has he now? Could of sworn he was out here chopping earlier."

"No, he wasn't. Dad wouldn't allow it. Aaron wouldn't bother asking anyway. He's probably asleep already. Damn good for nothing."

"He's alright. He helps out from time to time."

Reed lingered next to the fire and wiped sweat from his face.

Pale stars poked through the night sky and the moon hung like a mouldering pendant.

"Alright then, I'm gonna see how mom's doing. I might be back out in a bit," said Reed.

He walked from the fire while Jarrett sat and stared at his father.

Still he chops. The woods will be nothing but stumps before he's done enough work for the day, Jarrett thought.

Then he fixated on the fire, on the burning underbelly of the spiring flames.

The same stubbornness and the same restless pride in him is in me. But not in my brothers. They are like someone else. Maybe they are from someone else, he thought. Who knows what a woman hides. Love for another man, the seed of another man. Who knows.

He stood up and dug a rut into the dirt with his boot, back and forth, listening to the splitting wood against the moaning night and whispering flames. I must be of his flesh because I can't stop. Only with me it's not my body but my soul. I don't dream when I sleep, I think. I turn over the waste of days. Like some puzzle that can't be solved. I can't let it alone. Just like how he sits for a second and then he's up again, with a task for himself no one asked him to do. No one needs him to do.

Jarrett walked from the fire, the heat against his back, ghostly light cutting fluid shapes out of the ground. Down a dirt path to a wooden shed. He opened the door and lit a match. Rakes and shovels and a bench in the wan light. Leaves rustling, something scurrying; a rat or a mole. Jarrett turned and looked at the small hatchet and the long ax on the wall to his right. The curved wooden handle and the blade his father said was too dull to split wood.

Why won't he let up? Why doesn't he die? I'm getting into middle age. I feel like dying and he mocks me with his rusted grip on life. His face. His pupils like dull drops of paint. He works and works. It's his pride. My brothers have no pride. They sit around and pretend to work. They lift one finger and say they worked the whole day.

What do my mother and father see in each other? My mother sits at the window. She shrinks by the day and my father won't stay still. He won't sit in the house, he's always out inventing things to do that don't need to be done. And he holds it over our heads. He won't tell us he wants help and then he'll act like we're all lazy sonsabitches. When we try to help he says he doesn't need it and then he holds himself above us like he's the only one who works, the only one who knows what work is. I know what work is, I can't rest.

The match burned down and the flame singed his finger as he begrudged his brothers who didn't work hard enough and his father who worked too hard. Sloth and pride squeezing his wrathful brain. Standing in the dark he lit a match and walked to the wall. He grabbed the ax; dust floated and fell. From the shed he stomped onto the dirt. The fire had swelled.

Jarrett threw the match and listened for the splitting wood. The old man and his old bones. He must ache all the time but he won't say it, Jarret thought. The old man and his pride. A man and his sons born of woman's deceit. Imprisoned by the lies of love.

Why did my mother do it? Give herself to him and other men. How many other men? Shut up inside herself with her secrets. She sits in that damn window like an unlit candle. Why did she have us? She gave us life to watch her wither. They won't die until we're right behind them next to the grave.

The ax in his hand, Jarrett walked from the shed to his father and stood staring until his father looked back at him.

"Wanted to see if you needed any help. If you're going to keep cutting more wood, might be good to have a hand."

"No, no, I don't need any help."

The father went back to work. In the light from the monstrous fire, in the light now shellacking the yard and wall of trees, Jarrett stood in hellish relief.

He raised the ax. It seemed to hang in the air, in a space divested of time, as if in a still frame, as if it were not held by a hand of beating blood. He brought the blunt edge down on the back of his father's neck. The fire spit out beyond the rocks and scorched the grass. Jarrett chopped and chopped. It felt like cutting through a damp fallen tree and he was empty of thought for the first time.

THE ELEVATOR

THE MORNING OF HIS INTERVIEW Cliff had steel cut oats with goji berries. He got in the shower and turned the hot water on and let the steam swell and then he twisted the hot knob left and the cold knob right. The spout blasted him with freezing water and he screamed and shuddered and soaped himself and rinsed.

He turned off the water and stepped out of the shower, his teeth chattering, his skin textured like a basketball. Dried himself. In the fogged mirror he saw an infected ingrown hair under his lip.

"It doesn't matter, you have a good face. No one will notice. No one sees these things, no one cares," he said to himself.

Even though he saw the facial flaws of others: their pimples, moles, boils and rashes.

He lathered his face with shaving cream and grabbed his razor and guided it to his throat. The razor slid down his neck, plowing a path through sandalwood smelling cream. His hand shook but the shave felt smooth. The mirror was clearing up and he saw a fine red line on his neck. He put the razor down and ripped toilet paper off the roll and stuck it to the cut.

After shaving the rest of his face he got dressed. Silk boxer shorts and long black socks. Black slacks and a white dress shirt. He sat on the bed and put on new shoes. The laces were short and he barely had enough length to form a bow.

He stood up and felt a pinch in his pinky toe.

"Doesn't matter. Just need to break them in," he thought.

Wallet, keys, one last look in the mirror. Bloody toilet paper stuck to his neck. He pulled it off and waited. The cut had stopped bleeding. He grabbed a wad of toilet paper and stuck it in his pocket.

The halls of his apartment complex were unusually crowded. He took the stairs to the lobby and went outside. On the street he looked up directions to the interview. His trip would take forty-five minutes and he had three minutes to spare.

The skies were gray and the air was cool. Wind shook the leaves of plants and trees. People dressed in business casual clothes rushed down the sidewalk. A few men in stained sweatpants and torn t-shirts leaned on mailboxes and streetlights.

Cliff had to walk five blocks to the green line metro and take it to the Cardova Station and then get on the Blue line and take that to Little Czechoslovakia, and then he had to walk another three blocks to the Dynamicorp building.

The train smelled of spiced meat. He stood in the center gripping the handle hanging from the bar running along the top, leaning forward and backward when the train stopped and started, staring into the copper-colored neck of some slab of beef in front of him. Before he got off the train he saw a man eating a giant chili dog covered in diced onions.

Cliff walked as fast as he could. Smashed his pinky toes with every step. His calves burned. He worried about sweating. Unless a man is in the middle of a strenuous racquetball session, sweating is a bad sign, a sign of nerves, shame, weakness.

Every few minutes he pulled out his phone and checked the time and read a headline. Something about misallocation of funds in a war, a bridge that had collapsed, a teacher that had been fired for forcing students to do math.

"I should have given myself more time, I always do this" he thought.

With four minutes to spare he made it to the Dynamicorp headquarters. A chrome bullet-shaped building that imperiously shot up into the sky, as if violating its sanctity.

He walked into a cavernous lobby and checked in with a woman at a desk. She scrunched up her face and typed into a computer.

"Forty-seventh floor. A receptionist will direct you from there."

"Okay great."

He went to an elevator with shining doors in which he could see his shirt coming untucked.

"For the love of Christ."

He looked around and unbuckled his belt and undid his pants and stuffed his shirt into the pantlegs and zipped up and tightened his belt. Feeling like vacuum-sealed sausage, he pressed the button on the elevator.

A woman came up to his side and he caught her out of the corner of his eye. She looked good. Short and curvy. She wore a green blazer and pencil skirt. Her dark hair was up in a ponytail and she wore glasses and dull red lipstick. Cliff felt someone standing behind him and he smelled the chili dog from the train.

The elevator stopped on every other floor. Cliff checked the time. He waited and looked at the woman. Her eyes were on her phone.

There was a dinging sound and the elevator doors slid open soundlessly. Cliff started and stopped to allow the woman into the elevator. She started and stopped and waited for him to move. Cliff hurried into the elevator while saying sorry under his breath and damning himself in the innermost core of his being.

The elevator was enormous, like another lobby, and he had to take several steps to reach the back. When he turned he saw the man who'd been behind him, the man with the chili dog on the subway.

The doors slid shut and sealed Cliff in what felt like luminous doom. A giant metal box, bright and reflective.

The man walked into the elevator and looked at Cliff and turned and faced the door. He had impassive eyes, dim and gray. His arms were uniformly thick from the shoulders to the forearm. He wore faded blue dickies and a blue work shirt with a tag for his name. The space where his name went was empty. He carried a blue bag that bulged with what appeared to be heavy tools.

Cliff's voice cracked as he called out his floor. The woman said her floor and the man pressed the buttons. The elevator launched upward and Cliff whistled for a second and then ceased.

The climb felt like a fall into an inferno, as if hell sat atop the clouds. Cliff tried to think about his interview and remember his power poses and phrases. Firm handshake, not too firm. Eye contact, not too much eye contact.

On the thirty-fourth floor the elevator stopped without a sound. The doors stayed shut.

"Huh," Cliff said.

He looked at the woman. The man was silent. The woman let out a nervous laugh and looked at Cliff.

"At least the lights are on," Cliff said.

The woman laughed and held up her fist and coughed.

"Well, this is pretty strange, huh?" said Cliff.

"Yeah, this has never happened to me before," the woman said.

"That would be pretty crazy if it was a regular thing," he said.

"Yeah..."

"I'm supposed to be at an interview. I'm going to be late," Cliff said.

"You're interviewing for Dynamicorp?" the woman asked.

She looked him in the eye.

"Yeah, it's just an intern spot right now in the replication verification department, but I've been told it could be a pathway to a junior executive position."

"Wow, nice. Those spots are hard to get, from what I've heard."

"Yeah. It's all about networking. Knowing the right people. I got lucky. Do you work for the company?" He asked.

"I'm doing some consulting work for them right now. I'm actually going to be late for a meeting if we're stuck in here much longer."

Cliff got out his phone.

"Damn. I'm supposed to be on the forty-seventh floor in one minute," he said.

"Surely they'll understand. Getting stuck in an elevator of the company that's interviewing you is probably the best excuse in the books," the woman said.

"Hahaha yeah you're right."

Cliff reproached himself for his overeager laugh.

"What's your name?" Cliff asked.

"Christen,"

"I'm Cliff, nice to meet you."

He rocketed his hand forward like a punching robot. Her hand was small and soft and warm. He gave her a loose grip and two weak pumps and withdrew.

They looked at each other and fidgeted, scrunching up their toes and scratching their heads and smiling unnaturally.

"So, one of us should probably call someone," Cliff said.

"It looks like I don't have any service," Christen said.

"I don't either. That's weird."

"This whole building is supposed to be outfitted with the latest wireless technology. This building is practically a giant router," Christen said.

"Yeah, that's what I figured."

Cliff looked down and noticed his shirt bunched up around his waist like an inner tube.

"Are you fucking kidding me," he thought.

The man in the faded blue work clothes and the heavy bag stood with his back turned, wordless and obdurate.

"Well, there it is. I'm officially late to my interview," Cliff said.

"I can't believe we can't get service in here. This is outrageous," said Christen.

"Feels a little warm in here too. A little stuffy," said Cliff.

"Yeah, I wonder if something happened to the air circulation," said Christen.

"Are we not getting air? Are we going to suffocate in this box? I'm going to miss my interview and not get the intern spot, best case scenario. Worse case scenario I'm going to die a slow and agonizing death," Cliff thought.

"Well, I'm sure they have someone monitoring everything in the building. They have maintenance and security teams. I bet someone is on their way to fix it right now," he said.

"Yeah, I hope so. This is really weird," Christen said.

They looked at each other again and down at the silver floor.

"Where in the world do you not get service anymore? In a Dynamicorp elevator, of all places?" Cliff asked.

"It's not very dynamic, is it?" Christen said.

"Actually, in a way, you could say it is dynamic, because it's a change from the usual run of things. I bet that normally this elevator moves up and down the building without any variation in its functioning, but, maybe it's almost paradoxical, when it stops working, it introduces real novelty, and is therefore more dynamic than if it never broke down," Cliff said.

"Yeah, I guess."

The man moved to the side of the elevator. His steps heavy as if his boots were set in concrete. He put his back against the wall, slid down and sat with his knees bunched up to his chest.

"Well, all we can do is wait," Clifford said.

"My associate is going to be very upset that I'm not at the meeting. We were going over some very important material," said Christen.

"This is just unbelievable. Of all the things that could happen," said Cliff.

"It's definitely warm in here, I see what you're saying," Christen said.

"They gotta have someone working on the problem. They have a whole department that should be keeping their eye on this sort of thing," said Cliff.

The floors and walls and ceiling of the elevator gleamed and reflected their images. They stood against a background of shining nothingness, a sparkling void both limitless and entrapping.

"Jesus Christ. You try to do something. You try to advance your career and this is what happens. You get trapped in a fucking elevator with some freak who just sits there not saying anything, while this metal box cooks us like a microwave," Cliff thought.

The man leaned his head back against the wall and closed his eyes and cleared his throat. Clifford looked at Christen and then pointed a thumb toward the man and mouthed the words, "What's with this guy?"

She threw up her hands and got out her phone again.

"Still no service. It's been five minutes, at least," she said.

"I say we give it five more minutes. They'll have it figured it out by then," Cliff said.

His mind whirred:

"What are you going to do if it's not fixed, if you're still trapped in here? My stupid fucking shirt coming untucked at the waist. I knew that shirt would be a problem in the changing room. I could see it and feel it right there but I just wanted to get out of that department store. I have no patience for shopping. My shoes are too small. I'm going to lose it.

What's this guy's deal? Why doesn't he say anything? It's completely crazy. To go through all this and not say anything. How was he on the train earlier and now in the elevator with me? What was going on with that chili dog? Why did it have so many onions?"

"Man, I really hope they're understanding about the interview," Cliff said.

"Yeah. They're not exactly known for being lenient," Christen said.

"That's why I wanted to work for them. I wanted to be on a team with high standards. But this is their fault. If they give anyone a pass, it's gotta be me right now," Cliff said.

"You would think."

They fell silent and clutched an arm or shifted their weight or looked at their nails. A drop of sweat fell from Cliff's head and splashed on the floor.

"Whew. It really is hot in here. I'm starting to sweat pretty good."

Christen looked at him.

"Oh, nothing's wrong. I just sweat a lot. Always have. I come from a long line of sweaters. Not like sweater as in the garment. Haha, that would be funny. Sweaters as in people who sweat a lot. You should see my dad. That man. Wow. He used to play basketball with me, just the two of us. He always made time for me, even though he worked his ass off at the syrup factory. Man where does the time go? He was almost a young man then. He seems tired these days. Work really takes it out of you. Especially that kind of work. That's why I got those degrees. Education is the key, you know, the ticket to a better life. But when he bumped up against me, while driving to the basket, it was like I'd just jumped in a pool or something. He was wringing wet. I'm kind of like that too. Must be genetic."

"I think you're bleeding," said Christen.

His cut had opened and blood was running down his neck and staining the collar of his white shirt. Cliff put his palm to his neck.

"Oh shit. Sorry about that. Sorry, it's fine. It's really not a big deal. I cut myself shaving this morning. These blades they're making now. I think they've gone a little too far. They're a little too powerful. It's like shaving with a machete or something."

"Are you okay?"

"Oh yeah, it's fine. You probably don't know what this is like, but men cut themselves shaving all the time. Well, you shave too, I'm sure. Well, I don't want to assume. I'm not one of those guys that just assumes women should shave. I think we should be free to do what we want. If you didn't shave I would still find you attractive. As a person I mean. I mean I would respect you as a person."

Cliff reached into his pockets and pulled out a wad of toilet paper and held it to his neck.

"I thought something like this might happen. Good thing I brought along some toilet paper. It's triple ply and very absorbent. Should stop bleeding in a second. Wow it's hot in here," Clifford said.

With his hand pressing toilet paper into his bleeding neck, he looked at the man sitting against the wall. Christen stared at her phone.

"What is going on with this guy? He doesn't react to anything. How can he just sit there like that? What's in that bag? Looks like it could be tools, maybe wrenches and hammers. Is he working? Is he following me? What kind of a twisted scheme is this? What a lunatic. What an asshole. He's just going to let the tension build and not explain himself. Just come out with it already. Just fucking say something, do something, do something you bastard," Cliff thought.

He pulled the toilet paper off his neck, looked at the blood, turned the paper and dabbed his neck a few more times. Then he held out the bloody paper to Christen.

"See, not much there. Dried right up."

Cliff pointed to the cut.

"See? Good as new."

"Yeah. Glad you're okay."

"I've really lost her. It was going well," he thought.

He looked down and saw that his shirt had come untucked.

"Oh, will you look at that. My shirt came untucked. Man, I had really psyched myself up for the interview, but I'm not in much of an interviewing mood now. Whew," he said.

Christen smiled in the same way she would smile to appease a leering hobo.

Cliff unbuckled his belt and unzipped his pants while staring at Christen. The zipping sound rippled in the quiet.

"Don't worry, just tucking my shirt back in, putting everything back together. Not doing anything weird. Just want to be presentable here," Cliff said.

"It's okay. You're fine."

She turned away and looked at the glowing yellow elevator buttons. Clifford stuffed the bloody toilet paper into his pocket and shook his head again and flung sweat on the floor.

"Now I'm the one who looks like a lunatic," he thought.

"Just because I cut myself shaving. I'm writing to Trimco, I'm sending them an email and telling them to ease up on the blades, tone it down some. I guess I could just go with one of their older models. If they're even available anymore. Just because of this shirt that won't stay tucked in correctly. So I unzipped my pants. I didn't take anything out. It wasn't a sexual gesture. I had to get the shirt back in.

"This guy is driving me nuts. He has to be behind all this. He's orchestrated everything. He must have followed me on the street, got into the same train car with that chili dog. He followed me on to the elevator. He's out of his mind but now I look insane to this woman. I was going to ask her out. She was impressed that I was interviewing here. I could tell. I had her for a second. That's over now.

"What's in that bag? I don't remember seeing that on the subway. Could've been under the seat. Still, what's in it? Tools? For what though? Why doesn't he have a name on that tag? Maybe I'm just imagining this guy. Maybe it's the heat. The air in this room is so stagnant. It's not circulating. This can't be safe. I wonder how long before we get brain damage. We're going to suffocate in here," he thought.

Christen looked at Cliff.

"I think you're bleeding again."

"Oh, shit. That's crazy. Those blades, I'm telling you. Maybe I'll grow a beard. Save me some trouble every morning. I hear women like that look, too. Maybe that's what I should do," he said.

Cliff pulled the bloody toilet paper from his pockets and put it to his neck and then took it off.

"This toilet paper is used, it's no good. I need something else," he said.

He stood in the deathly air, his reddened and glistening face contorted into a clown portrait of thought.

"Don't mind me. This will be simple. I don't want to get more blood on my shirt. Normally I'd just use my shirt sleeve but I'm trying to look professional in case the elevator gets fixed and I can still make it to the interview."

Cliff bent over and untied his right shoe as sweat ran down his neck and stung his cut and mixed with the blood. His reflection stared up at him from the glassy underworld.

Cliff took off his shoe and sock. His pinky toe was red and

purple. The relief of freeing his pinched toe was immense. He exhaled loudly and stood up and put his sock to his neck.

"The way I see it, I can just go sockless. The interviewer won't notice I'm not wearing socks. But he'll definitely notice a bloody shirt," he said.

Christen looked at her phone.

"You may have noticed how bad my pinky toe looks. It's these shoes. They felt fine in the store. But they're too tight. They have too much of a taper. I thought the tapered look was sophisticated but this is just constrictive. My toe will be fine. Better to let it breath," Cliff said.

The man stood up with his back to the wall and leaned and picked up his bag.

"What's this guy going to do? For the love of Christ, just say something. Look at his hands. They're humongous. He could crush my skull with one of those things. I wonder if this is some kind of routine. Like he does this as a regular thing. Traps people in elevators and kills them," Cliff thought.

"Are you still not getting service?" Cliff asked Christen.

"No, I'm not getting anything. I don't understand this. It's getting so hot in here. I'm starting to get a little nervous."

"Yeah, I'm starting to feel a little funny myself," Cliff said, holding a synthetic dress sock to a razor wound on his neck, his right foot bare.

He pivoted to the man.

"Hey. What do you think of all this? This is pretty weird, right?" Cliff asked.

The man spoke:

"I try not to let things get to me."

Christen poked at her phone and Cliff stared at his shoe laying on its side.

The elevator shot upward. Smoothly, silently, inexplicably. It stopped on the forty-seventh floor and the doors opened, revealing a desk with a young blond woman at a computer. Cliff grabbed his shoe and looked at Christen.

"Well, maybe I can explain everything and still get an interview. It was nice meeting you."

"You too," she said, her eyes on her phone.

Cliff looked at the silent and stationary man. The doors were closing. Cliff ran and stuck his hand between them and they slid open. The woman at the desk glanced up from the computer as he walked out of the elevator. She smiled and her blue eyes twinkled.

AS I HANG DRYING

BELCH RESTAURANT REVIEW APP.
Porzio's Restaurant and Salami Shop
Average Rating: 4.5 stars.

Mike H. 5 Stars
One fine day I popped into this hidden little gem. Wow, was I in for a treat! I had no idea our humble little city was home to such culinary delights.

Porzio's has it all. From what I can tell, they are divided into three different sections. They have a full sit-down restaurant, a grocery, and then a separate section for salami. I have to admit it was a little confusing at first, because I just wanted a sandwich and didn't know where to go or how to order, but the employees were all so friendly and helpful, they cleared it right up for me. I must have looked like a real idiot wandering around, but they were not rude about it at all.

I'm pretty sure I talked to the owner, but it was all such a blur and I'm not sure if I remember his name. It could have been Porzio himself! A very large and very friendly bald man with a mustache talked to me for about twenty minutes. He was very eager to let me know that everything was made in house and that all the salami was cured in a special fridge in the back of the store. He made it sound so good and he was very passionate about his work.

I sat down in the restaurant and I couldn't help but notice how clean and sleek everything was. The menu was a little intimidating and they went into a lot of detail on the dishes. But I went with what I knew and got a pastrami on rye. The food came out fast. Holy moly that sandwich was so good. The meat was so tender and delicious and they used a house made thousand island sauce. And the house cut fries. I think they used their own lard, too.

After stuffing myself I didn't feel like shopping for groceries, but I'll be stopping by again sometime soon to pick up some salami and sauces. I can't recommend this place enough. Five stars.

Sophie P. 5 Stars
My girlfriends and I had talked about coming here for weeks. We heard the brunch was amazing. Last Sunday morning we were all a little hungover, to say the least, and we dragged ourselves to this charming spot in a neighborhood that is really up and coming. I've heard that the stabbings have gone down, so now is a good time to get in if you want to buy a house.

At first we went into the wrong part of the restaurant. It seemed more like a grocery store, with a lot of cases and coolers with fresh greens and meats. But the girl behind the counter was so nice and explained everything and before long we were seated. We were lucky to get the last big table because the place was filling up fast.

We started with a round of screwdrivers. They were boozy and we were having a great time. Our server was very informative. He had a story for every dish. The details were a little overwhelming but I'm sure you could learn everything you ever wanted to know about the food. We just wanted to get drunk and eat.

Two of the girls got the french toast with blueberry jam made from local blueberries. It looked so good and they said it was amazing. I got the chorizo skillet. It was so rich and creamy and delightful. Our other friend got the basic breakfast platter and it looked so good. We got another round or three of screwdrivers and watched the place get crazy busy. These guys are killing it.

From the food to the service to the décor, this place does everything right. The girls and I will definitely be back for another brunch. The grocery looks like it has a ton of options but we were all ready to go back home and watch some tv and pass out. Check this place out when you get the chance. Get here early for brunch or you'll have to wait.

Phil S. 5 stars

I am something of a salami connoisseur, an aficionado, if you will. Up until recently, I had been enduring the daily disappointment of living in a city without a world class salumeria. You can well imagine how pleased I was to discover a new market and restaurant opening in the old appliance district, which, before that, was a theater district and I believe a jazz alley as well. From what I hear, the area has undergone something of a renaissance, with boutiques springing up and far fewer street beatings than in years past.

On an evening unencumbered by official duties or social obligation, I strolled unaccompanied to Porzio's to gander at their goods. Now, I do believe that I blundered into the wrong portion of the establishment, for I seemed to be in a casual dining area, and I saw many plump guests sinking titanic sandwiches into their gastric depths. Alluring and intimidating as their meals were, I had an unwavering purpose: to sample the salami and purchase a stick or two if sufficiently impressed.

The elegant hostess was most helpful and directed me to my destination. Through a set of swinging doors I walked into a bounteous display of cured meats. I knew I had found my salami shangri-la.

The owner, sensing my appreciation for the craft, came out to greet me. We hit it off. I do believe that shared interests bridge the gaps of place, time, gender and race. But right off the bat, I had to put him to the test, and I can say with confidence that he passed. The man knows salami and loves it as I do. He regaled me with anecdotes. His knowledge of curing is surely up there with the world's finest salumists. I thought I knew a thing or two, but I would gladly put down good money to attend a course on curing if he were to teach it.

And then, for the centerpiece of my visit, the sample tour. I tried the sweet sopressatta. Balanced and mild, with an ever so subtle suggestion of garlic. I do believe I tasted red wine. Then the calabrese, with the perfect dose of calabrian pepper. Just spicy enough to light up the taste buds. Finally I tried Finocchiona, which had an enchanting licorice taste, provided by the fennel, no doubt. I have noticed that many people overdo the fennel, but not our master, here. He told me that he has crafted every salami recipe. I bought a stick of each of the salamis I sampled.

I am not an easily impressed man. In fact, I resist giving compliments as a general rule. But I cannot resist admitting that my expectations were exceeded by a considerable degree. Tommy Porzio, my good man, you have found a customer for life. Maybe even a friend, I will say. Next time I visit, after what will no doubt be another stimulating chat with Tommy, I will sit down for a proper meal at his restaurant.

Eliza M. 3 Stars

I have been hearing about this place and decided to check it out on my lunch break. Right off the bat, I walked up to the counter and tried to order one of their famous spank burgers and the woman at the register gave me an attitude. She was not nice at all. Apparently, I was in the wrong section and the restaurant was on the other side but they could have made things a little clearer.

When I finally figured everything out and sat down at a table, the server was nice enough and made up for the other woman. I ordered the burger and the fries. I don't know if they had a problem in the kitchen or what but it took forever. I sat and waited for over twenty minutes and it was not that busy. Maybe because they're still pretty new and they're working out some of the kinks. When the food finally came the fries were really hot and I burned my mouth but I guess that was my fault. I can admit the food was tasty. The burger was juicy and the fries were crispy and they gave me a cup of house made ketchup, which I thought tasted a little funny but that wasn't a big deal.

All in all, I think they have some pretty good food but the initial experience rubbed me the wrong way. They could stand to simplify things a little.

Rich A. 5 Stars

Have you ever eaten something that made you believe you could give up sex if you could keep eating that one thing? Before today I would have thought you were crazy for suggesting it. But right now, I'm here to tell you, if I could eat at this restaurant every day, I wouldn't care if I ever got laid again. It's that good.

The service was excellent. The interior was a little hipsterish, but they don't lay it on too heavy. They had a great selection of beer, too, with some selections from a few of the local breweries.

Just get the Hog Heaven sandwich. I'm thinking about it right now and I think I might have to go back and get another one.

Joe S. 2 stars

Frankly, I don't get what everyone's raving about. First of all, where do you go to order? It's a very confusing place. I ended up in the women's bathroom somehow. Sorry for whoever was in there. I'm not a creep. But speaking of creep, the owner gave off some very strange vibes. He's this absolutely huge man with a shiny bald head and a waxed mustache. He watches you with these piercing dark eyes and it's kind of scary.

I figured out how things work and sat down at the restaurant. Had a burger and it was nothing special. The ketchup tasted off. The whole place is just so over the top. I guess it's what the kids are into these days but I'm just fine with a nice meal at a Bud Sampson's, where the atmosphere is a little more down to earth. Color me old fashioned.

Sandy L. 5 stars

My husband and I had such a great time here! What a hidden gem. We couldn't believe the quality of the food. The meat is really different from what you get at other places. The staff is so friendly and knowledgeable too. My husband is hooked on the ham. He's mentioned it every day since we went, and that was two weeks ago! It couldn't have been a better date night. I'm sure we'll go again soon.

La'shwonda Q. 4 Stars

They got all kinds of meat and cheese. Friendly staff and a bunch of other grocery items too. The restaurant looked good, we just peeked our head in and it was busy. We walked out with some local maple syrup. We'll be back to try the restaurant side.

Buck B. 3.5 stars

Don't get me wrong, the food here is delicious. And the staff is pretty knowledgeable. But they keep saying this neighborhood is getting better and I just want to remind everyone that three people have gone missing in the last three months and the last place they were seen was in the same two block zone of this restaurant. They just disappeared. It's not a big story yet but keep your eyes open. Be careful if you're out walking or jogging in this area, it does not seem safe. They keep saying that all the beatings with the wooden boards have gone down and there haven't been any murders at all this year, but that's just what we know about. I say you should go as early as you can on a nice bright day and watch out. Oh and if you like salami make sure you get the calabrese, it's got just the right amount of heat.

Sam N. 5 stars

I'm getting on in years and my kids are all grown up and on their own now, and so one of my favorite ways to kill time is to check out the all the new shops and restaurants. Seems like every week there's a new place to go. It keeps an old man busy. Biggest mistake I ever made was retiring early, but Industrial Analytics won't take me back, they just hire young people now. You work your whole life looking forward to retiring and then you have too much time on your hands. But that's another story.

I've been meaning to try this little gem for a while and I'm glad I did. I went on a Tuesday evening and my first impression was that the staff was very friendly. They directed me to a table even though I believe I wandered into the wrong area at first. Afterwards I was able to see that they have several strongly worded signs out front with flashing arrows but I sure didn't see them when I first came in. I'd recommend one or two more signs or maybe a recording or a video that'll get people's attention.

I looked over the menu and asked the server a few questions and she was very knowledgeable about all the meats and how they're prepared. Seems they do just about everything inside the shop. She said they even do whole animal butchering in the back. Not many places like that anymore, I was impressed. I had a great uncle who was a butcher and that's a lot of work from what I can remember.

I ordered their signature cold cut sandwich, which is a whopping five meats and two cheeses, piled real high, with a house made dressing and local lettuce. It's got some serious flavor. I could barely fit it in my mouth. I think I can tell the difference with this meat being aged in house. Just something you can't get anywhere else. I took my time and even though they were pretty busy, nobody rushed me out. I saw the owner chatting with a couple people and he seems like a guy who's working hard and proud of his business. I might have to start a coffee shop or something like that and give myself something to do.

Layla L. 1 star

I didn't even end up eating here because of the unpleasant experience I had on the grocery side of the store. Part of the problem is that I wanted to order takeout from the restaurant but I couldn't tell where to go and I stood in the wrong line for like 10 minutes before I figured it out. Then this guy, who is supposed to be the owner I think, came out of some corner and, I'm not exaggerating, SCREAMED at one of the workers, something about not having enough olives. I don't really know what it was about but it was in front of a bunch of customers and we all just looked at each other like "uhhhh" and I just walked out. Bizarre.

Tad C. 5 stars

Tommy Porzio and the team bring consummate professionalism to our city's burgeoning restaurant scene. Not even ten years ago they were calling this a crud town but things have changed so much in the last few years. I can't believe it took me this long to make my way down to the old appliance district (they've really cleaned it up, I didn't see a single person face down on the sidewalk) to experience this hidden little gem. I could not have been happier with the whole experience. From the get go, I felt whisked away on a magical ride through an old-world butcher shop. It was like I was in Italy, for real. I could practically hear the organ grinder.

The staff is very knowledgeable, they really know their stuff. I like good meat but I don't mess with all the details. I'm more of a big picture guy. Well, I learned a couple things on my visit. I even had the owner Tommy hand cut a couple ribeyes for me. He was happy to do it, he pretty much insisted. He's sort of intense but I appreciate the dedication to the craft, as well as his passion for excellent customer service. He held onto the ribeyes and I treated myself to a late afternoon meal over on the restaurant side. I had one of their spank burgers, but I made it a double and added an egg. You can tell there's some extra love that goes into the meat. The flavors lingered in my mouth for hours.

I can see Porzio's being a really fun place to take a lady on a nice date. Maybe if I ever get one again I'll bring her here. (ha ha ha no really my number is 242-219-3497 no men please.)

Aaeyden. 4.5 Stars

My partner and I loved it. Our other partner and their partners loved it too. We went in a group of seven and Porzio's was more than happy to accommodate us. They moved a couple of tables around and everything was nice and comfortable. We felt safe and welcome the whole time. Now, three of us are vegans and two are vegetarians, so you might think there'd be no point in coming here, but that's where you're wrong. Porzio's has a wonderful selection of vegetarian and vegan entries. No one talks about it!

My partner and I had the FLT, which is for fakon (vegan bacon) lettuce and tomato. It was out of this world. Just delicious. The veganaise was creamy and tangy. Two of our other partners got a tofu hash scramble that looked and smelled incredible. Based on what they said, we will be getting that dish next time. And our two meat-eating partners said their sandwiches were fantastic. It looked like a lot of meat, if you can stomach that sort of thing.

I will admit, the salami section was not for me. I do not like to see dead animal flesh, especially when it's hanging. Despite their barbaric practice of slaughtering sensitive living beings, Porzio's is an inclusive place, and we will certainly return.

Mack B. 3 stars

You guys know that the owner's not Italian? His name isn't Tommy Porzio, it's Greg Landry. I mean, I get going for an aesthetic, and taking on the whole "old world" feel of a butcher shop in sicily or something, but that guy actually has people calling him a fake name. I just find it a little weird. His food is damn good, though, I'll give him that. Try one of the sloppy dogs, and make sure you have plenty of napkins.

Sharleen R. 5 stars

This place is unbelievable. Drop whatever you have in your hands and run down to Porzio's right this instant. You have never had food this good. Everything is prepared and served with such skill and care. The knowledge that goes into the food is off the charts. I feel blessed to live in a city with such an up and coming restaurant scene. I have heard that we are getting more attention from some of the really big name food critics (can't remember their names) and it's thanks to places like Porzio's. I have even read that chef Sam Silversting, a Jack Beardman award winner, is considering opening a restaurant here. That would really put us on the map.

But I'm getting ahead of myself. The food at Porzio's is too good. I came here with my boyfriend on a thursday night and we stayed for over two hours. I had the fall off the bone ribs, and I was falling out of my chair, they were that good. My boyfriend had the burger, which he made into a quadruple patty. They will stack it as high as you want. It looked amazing. The fries were just crunchy enough and everything tasted so fresh. I loved the local ingredients.

And I can't forget the service. It was just wonderful. Tommy Porzio is a standout talent. He does it all. He butchers, handles the groceries, designs the dishes in the restaurant, and he cooks. He really maintains a presence. It's a lot of fun to watch him running around everywhere. He talked to us for at least ten minutes, making sure we were having a good time and explaining his thought process on how he came to add certain ingredients. It was really informative and fun. Porzio's is one of those things you can point to as a reason why you stay in the city. Having access to this talent and passion makes bearing the traffic and wafting sewage smells worth it.

Buck B. 3.5 stars
I wanted to give an update on my previous review. Someone else disappeared while walking down Merton St not even two blocks from Porzio's. I think the city is trying to keep it hush hush because they want this area to thrive with all the new restaurants and shops and those big apartment complexes they keep building. But something is going on. I really would keep an eye out. Don't put in your headphones, stay aware.

***

From the notebook of Tommy Porzio:

It's funny. People say they believe in evolution. But they don't know what it means.

The meaning of evolution is that humans are animals, and that there is nothing more than blind survival. Another way to say it is that everything dies for nothing.

Over a hundred years after Darwin and we're still putting on this show about the sanctity of human life, as if we're higher than the rest of the natural world.

Men fill their fat bellies with pigs, cows and chickens; they sleep soundly after having gorged on roasted flesh. Yet they shudder at the thought of a man being eaten, they consider it a great indignity.

The horror of a man turned into a meal when he is no better than a pig.

Men say they believe in evolution because they don't want to be Christians. Their evolution is not about science or the truth, it is about denying religion.

They enjoy the convenience of not going to church, and the freedom to gratify their selfish impulses. But they still want the moral protection of religion. They still want to think they're special.

I have not heard one convincing reason why morality should still apply to our post religious world, to a world determined by chemical reactions and physical forces. We know that consciousness is an accident, something that never needed to arise. The conscience is also a fluke. Everything we think about right and wrong is arbitrary.

And as followers of science, we accept this. We tell ourselves that intelligence and consciousness are imperfectly developed tools in a pointless struggle for existence. There's no reason to live, no source of creation imbuing anything with value. There are only competing powers, temporary organizations of matter, lines of force, fluctuating fields of energy, relations among bodies moving at different speeds.

Nothing stands still, nothing endures. What you call a single person is a set of relations between many smaller bodies. What appears as one is a mixture of many, and when those many smaller parts no longer move and work together in the same way, the unity dissolves and the parts are assimilated by other mixtures.

So what makes a man different from a pig or a plant? He is a mix of bodies, a fleeting organization of matter. He has no soul. He has flesh and organs and bones and blood. Just like any other living thing. Just like any other living thing that we confine and slaughter.

Does anyone think pigs don't have feelings? That they're not aware of what is happening to them? That they feel no pain? We all know they do. But we also know that the pain doesn't last that long. The terror is temporary. We can block it out. But the idea of treating people like livestock, of raising and fattening them and harvesting their organs, is more than our tender-hearted Darwinists can bear.

I think they should be taught to bear it. They should be made to understand that it's not so different. We pride ourselves on our willingness to experiment, but I see so few experiments and so few experimenters. A man says he lives in a godless universe and what does he do? He jacks off or has an affair, and still feels uneasy.

I want to show what chaos entails. It's not just a subtle sense that life is meaningless as you go about your normal working day. It's not only making snide jokes about an impossible god.

It's anything goes.

THE MAN WHO COULDN'T WATCH TELEVISION

A HUSBAND AND WIFE. Good jobs with benefits, new house in a subdivision. The wife pregnant with their first child. She went to yoga for pregnant women and the dad bought tools. He tried to build a crib and bought one readymade soon after.

It was a normal pregnancy and a normal birth. A baby boy. The doctor ran tests. Later he said:

"He's healthy. Except it appears his eyes might have some sensitivity to light. It might be something we need to monitor."

The mom petted her baby's dark wet hair and forgot about what the doctor said. Her son was so chubby and wrinkled and beautiful. He would be fine. She would always take care of him.

They named the baby Bernard. The dad went to work at General Hydraulics and the mom stayed home. She held and rocked him and sang to him. Bernard lay on his back and kicked his arms and legs like an overturned turtle.

The first time he looked at a television he burped up milk. The mom cleaned it and set him down in his crib. A day later she put him in front of a television and he cried and puked. She cleaned him off.

Bernard grew and took teetering steps. Soon he was stomping on the beige carpet in the living room. Mom and dad smiling and laughing and following him bent at the waist with their arms outstretched, ready to stop him from running eyeball first into the corner of a coffee table.

Every time he looked at a screen he cried and puked. One day the dad yelled after Bernard hurled on an ipad.

"What's wrong with you?"

The mom said:

"He can't help it. It's his eyes. He's sensitive."

The dad sat there, ashamed and angry.

The mom worried. She talked to the doctor and he said:

"Looks like he's got some light sensitivity, doesn't seem too bad though. He might have a little trouble under certain kinds of light. We'll keep monitoring it."

In every other way the boy was healthy. He talked. He laughed and seemed happy. The couple decided not to have more children because of the economy and the state of the world. It would be irresponsible to create more life. And they had to take care of Bernard, who seemed to have a special condition.

"Is there anything we can do? Is there any medicine he should take? Or therapy?" The mom would ask the doctor.

He had no answers.

***

Bernard played outside and bounced balls which sometimes rolled down the driveway. The dad had to sprint after them. Bernard chased butterflies and poked at caterpillars and woolly worms. He went to preschool. One day when his mom picked him up, the teacher met her in the parking lot and spoke to her in a hushed tone.

"He had a little bit of an accident today. Twice, actually. He threw up when we watched Mr. Banana Man."

"Oh, he's very sensitive to those electronic lights. I'm sorry I forgot to mention that."

"So he can't watch any tv?"

"No, not really."

"What about a tablet? We like to use them for some of our lessons."

"He can't really look at those either."

The teacher was at a loss.

The mom took Bernard home and he ran around the sunbaked yard, waving a stick like a sword. He squatted and pulled tufts of grass from the ground and threw them into the air. The dad got home from work and got out of his Hyundai Santa Fe. With a worn out look on his face he said hello to Bernard and asked about his first day at school.

"It was great," said Bernard.

The dad went inside and saw the mom looking at her phone.

"Bernie says he had a good first day."

"The teacher told me he vomited twice."

"From the goddamn tv? They put him in front of a tv?"

"I guess."

"Well didn't you tell them about his problem?"

"I didn't say anything. I didn't know they would be watching tv."

"Is this just gonna be a problem for the rest of his life? How's he gonna get along in the world?"

"He'll be fine. We'll figure something out. We'll keep seeing doctors. We'll find a specialist."

Bernard cried on the bus. He was considered neurodivergent with individualized educational needs. But he loved playing outside. His parents got him a golden retriever named Samson. The boy and the dog went on long walks.

Schools used tablets and iPads. They assigned digital courses. Bernard did all his homework on paper. His teachers said his digital fluency was in the first percentile.

His dad did his best. He threw a football to Bernard and bought a basketball goal and hired a crew of dumpy men to lay concrete for a big court in the backyard. His mom took him to eye specialists and neuroscientists at university hospitals. They gave her conflicting information. Some insisted nothing was wrong. Others said he had minor blue light sensitivity and that it would disappear in time. Still others said he had a year or two to live at most.

His mom woke up before dawn and logged on to the internet. She read message boards and abstracts of medical papers. Tried to find an online community. Most of the people she read seemed a little unstable.

His dad woke up early but he went into the basement and watched tv before work. He was promoted to assistant supervisor of technical administration. With the money he bought a motorcycle and went for rides on the weekends. His health benefits allowed Bernard to go to the best doctors who laughed and shook their heads at what other doctors said.

As the seasons spun around and life became a blur of falling leaves and snow and sweltering summers, Bernard grew into a young man with an interest in veterinary medicine. His dog Samson was getting older and Bernard wanted to find new treatments for his hip dysplasia. His classmates talked all the time about the shows they watched. They shoved their phones into each other's faces and traded videos of people dancing and images with nested references to other images. Sometimes they forgot about his condition and showed him a screen and he puked.

Bernard got a girlfriend the summer of his senior year. The girl had long blonde hair and brilliant blue eyes. They were both shy and had talked all year without touching. One night she invited him over for a swim after her parents had gone to sleep. The water gleamed in the moonlight and the pool pump hummed, crickets chirped. They faced each other in the gently rocking pool. The pupils of her eyes grew wide and shimmered like black gems, drew him into her.

They kissed and held each other in the water until their skin shriveled. The rest of the summer was theirs and they started their senior year as a couple. But she graduated early and went to a prestigious school on the coast. She called less and less and then broke up with him over text.

His dad put a hand on his shoulders and said it would get better and that he would find someone else, but who really understands women anyway. On lambent evenings Bernard fell into bed and cried into his pillow. He graduated and went to veterinary school, though he stayed at home to save money.

On afternoons and evenings when everyone was watching tv or playing on their phones he would walk around or look out the window and let his memories and feelings glide over each other. He looked into the world and looked into himself and he couldn't tell where one ended and the other began. Sometimes it was like floating and sometimes it was like sinking.

He heard people laughing and talking about what they'd seen. People thought he was quiet. When in mixed company he smiled and nodded his head and said he'd heard of the shows, had seen an episode or two. His dad made a visual media study guide for him, described the popular programs and characters and wrote plot outlines in a notebook.

No one knew by looking at him that he'd never watched a show or a movie. He appeared as a normal man, a man who, like any other, spent countless nights letting waves of blue light wash over him. While waiting in offices or sitting on park benches or walking down the street, he stuck out because he didn't stare at his crotch or run into fire hydrants and street signs while texting his friends, but because everyone else had their heads down, no one noticed.

He could pass as a television watcher and phone user in casual conversation with acquaintances, but when someone invited him over or tried to share media with him, he had to tell them about his condition.

"Huh, that's crazy," they said.

"So you can't watch anything at all. You can't use a phone?"

"Nope."

"So how do you know what's going on in the world?"

"I read newspapers and magazines," he said.

Sometimes whoever he was talking to said:

"I kinda wish I had that condition. I'd probably be better off if I couldn't use a phone."

Within seconds they had their phones out.

A few of them held out longer. They stopped and tried to concentrate.

"Can you listen to podcasts?"

"Yeah, I can. But I don't."

" Why not? You listen to music?"

"Sometimes. I have to get someone else to play it for me though. I don't like to bother people."

"But if it's on, you can hear a tv playing and it doesn't make you sick, right?"

"Yeah, I could listen to it. I usually don't, though. It doesn't really work if I can't see what's going on. I like to be able to see."

"So any light from a tv at all will make you puke?"

"As long as I don't look at the screen directly I won't vomit. But the light always makes me a little nauseous."

"How do you get around, though? Do you use a GPS?"

"I use a map."

They could not believe it, that here was a man trapped in another time. The same flesh and blood as them, the same outward signs of humanity, but something unknown behind the eyes, a light beaming from a realm empty of televised images. But even their wonder lacked fire, and they forgot the oddity before them.

Bernard graduated from veterinary school and moved to an apartment in a small city an hour away and got a job in a clinic. His boss was a kindly old man with bushy white eyebrows and messy white hair whose face broke into a thousand creases when he smiled. The clinic was busy and Bernard loved taking care of sick and injured animals. He treated dogs, cats, bunny rabbits, birds, gerbils and other assorted rodents. On any given day at work, he could be seen wearing a white lab coat and a stethoscope, listening to a hamster's heart.

Not every case was a success. A lump formed in his throat when he had to tell the family. Samson got older; he had a snowy snout but he lay on the hardwood floor of the apartment looking as happy as ever. When he got up he took slow shaky steps one paw at a time. Samson gave out one winter. Bernard buried his only friend in a pet cemetery.

With no dog and no woman, he devoted himself to his work and spent his free time reading books on animal medicine. When he tired of reading about medicine, he went to the library and checked out books on ecology. Then he developed an interest in rocks and geographic history and stocked a spare room with geodes.

One day his boss said to him:

"I'm going to retire and I want you to take over my practice."

"I'd be honored. I don't deserve it."

"Sure you do, Bernie. Of course you do. You know what you have? An uncommon intensity. A focus, a love for the field. A love for what you do. I've never seen anything quite like it."

"It's my condition," Bernard said.

"Yes, that makes some sense. I'm sure that's had an influence. Have they made any progress on figuring out what's going on?"

"No one knows anything."

"Sometimes the experts don't always know what they're doing or what they're talking about. I'm sure not being able to look at screens has freed you up some. Maybe that's why you're so focused. I am an old man now, but I was born into a world with television. It's hard to imagine what it was like before."

"We can never know. Not even me. Everyone around me is watching something all the time. I have to interact with these people who speak a language I barely understand," said Bernard.

"Yes, you're right. I don't think any of us can wrap our minds around it."

And that was it. They talked about business. They talked about how Bernard would take over the clinic.

The boss retired and Bernard ran the clinic with skill and warmth. People travelled from a hundred miles away to see him. Women flirted and asked him out. If they wanted to walk in a park or go for a hike, sometimes he said yes. When they asked him to come over and sit in the dark before a streaming service, he backed off.

Nature was his life. When he wasn't working, he waded in rivers and hunted rare rocks, he left boot prints in woodland muck. At home he roasted chicken and duck and drank wine.

Sometimes he sat in his chair or stood in the middle of the room and looked at the walls or the ceiling or stared at the floor by his feet. Wondered what it was like to watch television, to use a phone. He never knew if he was happier than everyone else.

His parents aged and his dad bought a big flat screen television that almost spanned the living room wall. It was like a theater. The old man sat in his recliner and kicked his feet up. He looked through the options on his streaming service for hours, and sometimes fell asleep in front of the menu screen, his head leaning back and his mouth open, the music so loud it shook the windows.

Bernard visited and they sat and talked for twenty minutes and then silence overtook them.

"Well, I'm going to watch something now, I think," his dad said.

Bernard nodded and said he loved them and went into his old room. He looked at the bed with the crisply tucked sheets. He sat on the bed and the springs groaned. Then he went back into the hall and called to his dad from around the corner.

"Okay, think I'll be heading on out now."

The tv was too loud and his dad didn't hear him so he shouted.

"Oh, sorry son. Didn't hear you," said his dad.

His dad turned off the tv and pushed in the footrest of the recliner and lifted himself out of the chair. His mom got up from the couch and hugged him.

"You come back anytime," she said.

"Okay, I'll let you know when I can visit. I'm really busy."

"Oh we know. You're doing so well for yourself."

Years later Bernard went to the pound and adopted a new dog. Another golden retriever, a one-year-old who had turned up at a fish fry. The dog had knocked over a table full of catfish and a fat man in an apron tackled him. Bernard named the dog Thales and brought him home and trained him.

A war broke out overseas and there was talk of revolution making its way back here. People at his clinic barely said hello before they condemned a political party or the president. They talked about racial unrest and a history of oppression. Everyone was talking about a financial crash and a housing bust and speculative bubbles. After that it was the environmental crisis and the threat of superbugs, both germs and mutant insects breeding in radioactive habitats and acquiring bullet proof shells and pincers that could cut through a steel beam.

Bernard stopped reading the papers and magazines. When people wanted to talk about events, he would say:

"I know, it's really terrible what's happening. It makes you wonder."

Each evening he read classic literature by lamplight with Thales by his side. Bernard was getting on in years himself, and despite the dreamy and mystical look in his eyes he appeared fresh-faced. The secret was the soundness and depth of his sleep. When it was time to sleep it was like gently kicking a boat off the shore and gliding over placid waters. His dreams were vivid but mostly peaceful.

Every morning he went to the window in his bedroom and watched the birds and squirrels, looked over the dewy grass and then peered into the sky. Studied the sunrise. He took Thales for a walk and each time it reminded him of his childhood with Samson.

Being in public was hard. Televisions covered the walls of bars and restaurants. One look and he might retch in the middle of a conversation, between bites of fancy French fries. People didn't understand. Out in a grassy expanse where dragonflies chased each other, there was no need to limit his vision.

His clinic attracted the top veterinary talent in the state. An intern came from India. Bernard stepped back from his practice, gave more tasks to the other doctors and assistants. They maintained the standard of excellence well enough, though no one else had quite the same passion or focus.

When his dad died he moved his mom into his house. When she died two years later, Bernard retired from his clinic. He sold it to a veterinary conglomerate. Thales had grown old as well. The weary dog lay at the foot of Bernard's bed all day and night.

"Soon it will just be me," Bernard said, looking at the dog's clouded eyes.

Thales lived another year and then Bernard buried him in the same cemetery where he'd laid Samson to rest.

Though he had never been interested in such things before, Bernard bought a classic car and went on trips. He stayed in hotels at night and drove all through the day. Stopped at ridges and looked out over misty wooded gorges. Climbed up and sat in the world's largest rocking chair.

After a year of road trips, Bernard returned home. He sold his house and moved into a condo on a lake, where he sat on the back porch and looked out with dimming vision on the shining surface of the water. His bones ached and his chest hurt when he breathed and when he died it was like kicking off the shore.

STATE OF NATURE

HE LAY FLAT ON HIS FACE, breathing into the upturned ground. It was a sunny day blackened by gun smoke and dust clouds. The earth shuddered and spewed red clay. Exploding artillery shells sent flaming steel through sagging flesh all around Private Preston Tater. He'd lost contact with his squad leader. His platoon had been pinned down in an open field and torn to pieces.

Tater had been fired at before, but this was the first time he had seen the shredded guts of his fellow soldiers. He wanted to flatten himself into a sheet. The fear was unlike anything he'd ever felt. And he'd felt and done much in his sixty-six years of life.

The youths of every society in the world had taken power, and they reorganized warfare as a way of culling the old. A man was eligible for the draft on his sixty-second birthday. The generals were all between twenty and thirty years old. At thirty, men were cleared for clerical work and reproduction. At age forty-five, they were put into factories and forced into dangerous manual labor.

The politicians were between ten and twenty years of age. Upon turning twenty, each person was given a choice between a decade of leisure or public service. Most opted for the ten years of casual relationships, artistic dabbling and recreational athletics.

In the old days, the young had been sacrificed in ritual and war. At the beginning of their rule they decided that the traditional arrangement was irrational. Though the elderly made poor soldiers, with their brittle bones, weak hearts, hobbled gaits and sagging skin, the young elite thought it was more reasonable to slaughter those who could no longer enjoy their bodies.

Tater had a bad back, bad knees, bad eyes and bad ears, so he was assigned to the infantry as a rifleman. This was the first big battle of a recently declared war. After ten minutes of pressing himself into the flesh-peppered earth and hearing the groans of his dying friends, he resolved to move. He looked back and saw the bodies of old soldiers heaped and broken, he saw a trail of dentures and spectacles, prostheses and orthopedic undergarments and fiber supplements and laxatives and antilaxatives behind him. The only way was forward.

Up ahead about two hundred yards, Tater saw a concrete bunker with a slit in the middle. He crawled as fast and as low as he could, over rocks, pebbles and pools of blood. Bullets zipped overhead and pelted the dirt all around him. He made it to the base of the hill where he flipped onto his back.

"Tater, are you okay?"

It was Sargeant John Halehorn, sixty-three years old, Tater's squad leader. He was the only man who'd reached the hill.

Halehorn charged out ahead of his men but every other member of the squad except for Tater had been blown apart.

"Yeah, I'm not hit. I'm fine."

"Okay, good. We should be able to flank this bunker, take it from behind."

"Yes sir."

Halehorn crawled around Tater and got up into a crouch. Tater followed Halehorn up the hill around the side of the bunker. Tater let Halehorn run a few feet, stop and signal back to him. About halfway up the hill, Tater saw an enemy soldier pointing his rifle at Halehorn. Though his reflexes had slowed, he was fast enough to bring up his rifle and fire in time. The enemy soldier jerked like a puppet on a string and then he crumpled to the ground, one boot angled up in the air. Tater had never shot anyone before.

"Good work private. He just about smoked me," yelled Halehorn.

Tater and Halehorn got to the top of the hill. The bunker lay ahead a few yards. Halehorn crept forward, hunched, rifle outward. The machine gun in the bunker continued firing in short bursts onto the field below. Halehorn threw his back against the concrete and slid toward the edge. He leaned his head back and then grabbed a grenade, pulled the pin and lobbed it around the corner into a small open doorway. The grenade went off and the machine gun stopped firing.

Halehorn signaled to Tater to fan out and flank the bunker. Tater moved sideways, pain running through his hips and knees. His joints were acting up again but he kept moving. He saw Halehorn dart through the opening and vanish into the dark. No gunfire or sounds of struggle.

Out of the dark doorway Halehorn emerged, looking tired. He gave a thumbs up sign.

"They're dead as can be."

"Trouble is we lost our radioman."

"Do you know if he's dead or just stuck on the field?"

"Parts of him are scattered all over that field."

***

At the forward camp they established on the hill, Tater sat on an ammo crate and ate Salisbury steak. Thin brown sauce dribbled onto his chin. A few men sat around him, eating, staring off into space.

Patrick Berry, eighty years old, hobbled to a crate next to Tater.

"Seat taken?"

Tater shook his head.

Berry eased himself down onto the crate and whistled.

"We got hit real hard today didn't we?"

"I got reassigned to a new squad cuz everyone in mine is dead except for Sarge."

"Lieutenant Andrews is dead, too. We're getting a new platoon commander. Might be Halehorn is what I heard," said Berry.

They sat in silence for several minutes. Tater chewed and swallowed the last of his spongy steak.

Berry looked up and saw Tater wince.

"It's not exactly home cooking."

"No, no it isn't."

"Let me ask you something. You think this is right? Is this the way things oughta be?" Tater said.

"What do you mean? You talking about the war?"

"Well, yeah, the war, but the way we do it. Making the old ones fight it and do all the dying."

Berry hung his head and rubbed the back of his neck with his hand. He said nothing for a minute. An army truck rolled by.

"It's not for me to decide. There's way too much wrapped up in it, too many interests, it's way too far back now, you know?"

"It wasn't always like this. If you study history, you read about how things used to be the other way around. It was the twenty-year olds who did the fighting. It's only been this way for a couple hundred years now. In the whole scope of time that's not that long," said Tater.

"No, I suppose it isn't that long. I'm eighty and sometimes I don't know how to feel about how long life is. Some days it feels like I've been alive forever, other days it feels like I just got here. I do know life used to be better for me," said Berry.

"I don't think it's right to be fighting at this age. We should take it easy."

"You know how it works. We fight and die cuz our bodies aren't any good anymore. It's not as much of a waste. Think back when you were twenty, you remember how much fun you had? I was at the beach all day. I chased girls, I didn't have a care in the world. I can still remember it," said Berry.

Tater threw his can of steak and wiped his mouth on his stained wet sleeve.

"I used to paint, I got pretty good with all that time I had," he said.

"Now imagine if instead of painting, when you had all that time and energy, you had to do something like this? Wouldn't that be a waste?"

"I don't know. This doesn't seem right either. You read history and they used to value things differently, it's hard to explain."

"Explanations don't matter much. That's one thing I know. When the body starts to fail, might as well work, might as well fight, might as well die. Our time is over."

Berry looked at Tater and went on:

"No sense in being selfish, we've had our fun. We're doing this so the younger generations can have theirs. Plus, you know how much more terrifying this would be when your senses are sharp? You ever have kids?"

"No, I never had them."

"Well, I got two kids and three grandkids. I'll tell you what.

I'm happy to be here in their place. My grandkids are in their twenties, living the way they're supposed to live. Having fun, doing whatever they want."

"I guess," said Tater.

"Everybody wants the fun to last forever. But it doesn't."

Tater braced himself against the crate and got up. He felt something snap on the right side of his hips. He nodded at Berry and limped off toward a big green tent thirty yards away. Berry said something else but he couldn't hear it. Inside the tent was a long metal table and a man of about thirty seated beside two older men. They were passing sheets of paper back and forth and talking.

Tater stood and watched the men, waiting for them to notice him. The heat of high noon radiated; the sounds of marching soldiers and crunching tank treads whirled around him.

"Sir, permission to speak."

The younger man, Brigadier-General McBradley, a decorated veteran commander, was nearly too old to lead. He had begun his career at twenty-one, as a field marshal commanding the army in the last major war. Now he was finishing his career at the head of a brigade.

"Permission to speak."

"What is it, private?"

"Sir, with all due respect, I strongly advise against further frontal assaults until enemy positions have been sufficiently weakened by combined air and artillery strikes."

"That's by the books, private. Every assault is preceded by a shelling and bombing intended to rip apart the enemy's butthole. There's no free lunch and there's no free war. Men are going to die."

"Yesterday I saw whole platoons get wiped out for one hill. We could have prepared better."

One of the older soldiers next to McBradley looked up at Tater and raised an eyebrow. The other solider lowered his head and shuffled papers.

"Whole platoons. You may have noticed we have many, many platoons for the very purpose of losing them. You survived the battle, you won another day and you come to me to complain about how I'm handling this war? Private, I'm going to close my eyes and count to five and when I open them, I better not see you standing here in my tent because if I do, I will personally strap you to a rocket and launch you right at my next target. Do you understand?"

"Sir, yes sir."

Tater's swift saluting motion made his elbow joints pop and crack. He turned and marched out of the tent. His first step out brought him right into the face of another soldier, Private Shaw, an old man of eighty-six.

"Tater, what are you doing?"

"I was just giving my feedback to the general."

"Surprised you're still alive."

"Surprised any of us are."

Private Shaw was one of three surviving members of the platoon that led the charge in yesterday's battle. In his youth he was known for his sexual appetite. He had genital warts but no children. Then he worked in an LCD factory for thirty-five years and when he was old enough for combat, he found himself serving in front-line units on dangerous missions. The memories of his passionate youth had been swallowed by twenty-six years of flesh-grinding and bone-melting horror. He sometimes wondered if it had been worth it.

"You know we got another hill to take. Gonna be suiting up for it here at fourteen hundred."

"Is that right?"

"It's what I heard."

Tater looked up into the blue sky and forgot that he was talking.

"Heard it's gonna be even worse than the last one," said Shaw.

"Might as well be. Don't know why we bother with all of this."
Tater walked away from Shaw and went back to his ammo box. Barry was gone. Soldiers marched by and squatted or sat on crates and ate gray slop from rusted tin cans. They smoked cigarettes and stuffed oily wads of tobacco into their mouths. They rubbed balms on sore muscles and wrapped their aching joints in gauze, they spit and spoke obscenities. Tater looked on life between battles as a mocking dream. Soon most of these men would be dead. Soon he would be dead.

In the past, when young men fought, they looked beyond war, they looked forward to growing up and growing old and watching generations come up behind them. The paradise of the everyday awaited them. They had girls, young wives and young children. A nation ready to receive them as heroes. Certainly much to lose, but so much to gain, so much to remember and want while they crawled through the mud.

In Tater's time, he and his fellow geriatric soldiers had much less to look forward to. They had nothing left to enjoy if they survived.

Many young men were sacrificed in the past, doomed to a violent death by the vainglory of commanders and the madness of tyrants, but there were also rules of engagement, levels of prudence, degrees of regard for the flower of youth and the future of a nation. But men of Tater's age were the wilted petals and dry leaves of the past, they were a problem, a nuisance, clutter and crap, something to sweep away and burn into nothing. In the wars of the old days, leaders balanced aggression with caution. Now the conductors of war gave little thought to preserving some politically expedient percentage of their soldiers. As some were bold enough to say, the more dead the better.

Private Shaw had returned to the camp where Tater sat and thought about the ugly end of his days.

"Tater, you alright? You got that thousand-yard stare."

"Yeah, just thinking."

"Well, I'd advise against that. Sometimes thinking is worse for your brain than a bullet."

"If only."

"Hey, let me ask you, what are you gonna do when this is over?" Tater asked.

"If I make it, you mean?"

"Yeah, if you make it."

"I've been through a few of these already. But I don't think I'm coming home from this one. I got a bad feeling about it. This next battle. This next hill, I'm gonna get it," said Shaw.

"What did you do before, when you went home?"

"Not much. There's not much for an old man to do after he's spent his youth."

"I've been thinking of how it used to be different. If you look at history, if you go back far enough, you can see how different it used to be," said Tater.

"Was it better? How would we know?"

"I'm not saying I know it was better. But there was this idea, they called it wisdom. Old age had value because living a long time meant you could teach people something, you could help the young understand how to live," said Tater.

"Seems backwards to me. The young know how to live, they have energy and creativity. That's what all knowledge comes down to. They can run and jump and fuck. There's not too much more to it than that. And I can't hardly do any of that anymore, so here I am."

Shaw scratched his withered ass and closed his eyes. He seemed to fall asleep standing up.

"Shaw."

"Just dozed for a second. Well, not a whole lot of sense thinking about it. We're not gonna change anything. I'd say get in a good meal if you haven't already. Might be your last."

***

He stepped over freshly fallen bodies. Through the wafting clouds of sulfurous smoke he saw an inchoate shape stagger through the bloody mire. He kept moving, his hip joints screaming with pain. Each step risked death by bullets and bombs. He wanted it to end.

But Tater was also aware of some contrary spiritual pressure, an animating power which pushed him on through a hailstorm of lead as his fellow soldiers gasped and tumbled and stained the blackened earth with their blood. Something in him wanted life, ever more life, even in old age, in decrepitude, servitude, in terror and stink and shit.

If he could survive the war, then he could start a movement, a revolution, or maybe it would be called a restoration. He could lead degraded elders back to a place of respect. But it had to be done without more violence. The war machine had to be stopped. No one should die to stimulate the economy or increase national prestige. Everyone should be free to live, even free to do nothing, to be useless and unnoticed, to be quiet and content without getting yanked from the peaceful stream of life and yoked to a madman's murderous ambition.

Tater imagined a future without war as he trudged across a cratered field topped with body parts; he dreamed of attending classical music concerts as bullets whizzed within an inch of his ears. A different world, a world in some ways like the distant past, but in other ways like nothing that had ever come before. Where the young looked up to the old and listened to their advice, where disputes would be settled with rational argument and compromise. He was out ahead of everyone, or the only one left, marching into a field without holes and blasted earth, without corpses or men flailing and crying for their long-dead mothers.

He saw stacked sandbags and black barrels on the horizon. The yellow flashes of firing guns like lightning bugs on a dusky summer evening.

DAWSON ST.

EVERYONE GOT UP and walked out at the same time. We'd been eating in silence, hunched over paper plates on long gray tables. The food was dry and bland, like chewing on erasers. Chicken strips and french fries, not enough salt. No ketchup or ranch.

Out in the parking lot we staggered to our cars. The sunset burned at the bottom of the sky like a dying fire.

Shoes scraped the ground, scattering pebbles. Lighters flicked. I heard a few coughs. Didn't hear anyone crying. No one had cried since the service. People got into their cars without saying goodbye. Maybe they waved or nodded, I didn't see it. Car doors shut and crickets chirped. Tiny wings and legs all around us. We were in a bowl of bugs.

Engines started, old Celicas and F-150's, unmuffled. I didn't recognize most of the people at the service and the reception. Maybe we went to high school together and I couldn't remember them.

A lot had happened in fifteen years. At the same time I had a feeling that not enough had happened.

Becky came out of nowhere. She rubbed my arm and walked beside me until we got to the car and then she opened the passenger door and stood there staring at the beige building on the other side of the lot. It was a strip mall with a vape shop and a thrift store and a Chinese restaurant.

I turned and saw Clayton with his little girl Jane. She had dark sauce on her face, looked like barbecue. Not sure where she found that, I never saw any sauce.

Clayton nodded at me, seemed like he wanted to talk. But I didn't want to. I hadn't had anything to say all day. The ceremony didn't comfort me.

The preacher kept saying Jonny was in a better place. I don't believe it. Never did believe that kind of talk. There's no better place than this one, and this place isn't all that great.

"Go on ahead and get in the car, I'm gonna find mom real quick" I said.

"You gonna say goodbye to Ann Marie?" she said.

"I think she left. I didn't see her at the reception. Did you?"

"Yeah, she was over by Ray and Tammy. You didn't see em?"

"Nope. Could've sworn none of them were there. Not many of Jonny's friends even showed. Don't feel like I know this town anymore," I said.

"Don't be talking like that. You don't need to make it worse," she said.

"You just wait here a second. I'll find mom."

I walked past Clayton and Jane and cut between a couple other people I've seen around town. Maybe we used to hang out in parking lots and sit on tailgates or in lawn chairs around bonfires on cool nights in the fall. It had all blurred like rain on glass.

Cars pulled out and turned onto the road. I waited for the door of the home to open. No one came out.

I went back to my car. Becky was in the passenger's seat on her phone, smoking a cigarette. I got in and started the car and put on the radio. Twisted the dial until I hit a good country station. The latest Buck Chapman tune.

Becky and I wouldn't talk the whole ride home, probably the rest of the night. It wouldn't be until tomorrow morning, when I'd be getting ready for work and she'd have the news on or some other program. One of us would say something about what was on the tv.

I knew I'd be thinking about Jonny for a long time. Blame myself and everyone else, him too. I'd think about what I could've done to stop this. We believe things could've turned out different. That's what makes life so hard to bear. Especially when it goes on and on like it does for most of us.

***

Some nights I like to drive north to the city. Before leaving I'll smoke a bowl or two, take a hydrocodone. Bring a six pack of beer. Country roads, then the interstate. Usually not much traffic. When I get to the city I'll drive around for an hour, stop at a taco truck or a chicken place.

This was one of those nights. I was two beers deep, just starting to buzz. Late summer night, perfect with the windows down. Passing cars sounded like waves hitting the shore. Brake lights blazing red and then switching to dull silver, stoplights blinking those bright colors.

On nights like this I try not to think too much. I'm not a smart man. But even a stupid man is hounded by his tireless mind. It's not that he doesn't think enough, it's that what he thinks about is to no purpose, or contrary to what purpose he has.

I needed to go see Jonny. I'd been putting it off. My own brother living a few neighborhoods down and I don't take the time to drop by. Should do it once a week. Family is the most important thing in the world. You take it for granted. Get caught up in your own troubles, your own dreams.

Jonny's been going through some stuff. I worry about him. He might think I could care less. We don't see what someone else thinks, we only see what they do.

He'll be okay, though. He's got Ann Marie, he's got Mom. Good women in his life. That consoles a man for just about everything. It's done a lot for me. I don't know what I'd do without Becky. If Jonny didn't have Ann Marie he'd be in a real tough spot.

***

Mom was at the table. On the table was a crumpled black purse. A stained plate, some syrup shining in the light from the ceiling fan. An ashtray full of smashed butts like planes that had taken a nosedive.

"Dale around?" I said.

"He's out back, working on something," she said.

"He's always working on something, isn't he?"

"That's what I like about him. Not like your dad," she said.

"He had his strengths."

"You don't even remember him."

"I remember some things."

I stood by the sink and waited for mom to talk. It was quiet in the house. Birds were singing outside. I opened the cupboard and took out a mug and went to the coffee maker and poured a cup.

"Becky doing okay?" she said.

"Yeah, yeah, she's alright."

"You two getting along?"

"Bout as good as ever," I said.

"That's good."

The coffee steamed into my face. Didn't need more caffeine. Already had a Bull Blast energy drink. But I love the sensation of drinking coffee, its bitterness, its heat. In the morning it's nice to feel the jitters, like something big is about to happen.

I sipped the coffee; it burned my tongue.

"You seen Jonny?" Mom said.

"Not for a second."

"Well, you should go over there. He's still not working. I told him he's gotta get up out of the house. It's not right for him not to be working," she said.

"What about that tech school program he was talking about?" Mom took the plate to the sink and set it down.

"I don't think anything came of that," she said.

"Well shit. Think that'd be a good opportunity for him," I said.

"You should go tell him that. Maybe he'll listen to you."

"Figure it's a little late for that," I said.

"Not until it is."

I sipped the coffee.

"You gonna stay awhile?" Mom said.

"I don't know. Maybe until lunch. I got shit to do today," I said.

Mom walked to the table and pulled a pack of cigarettes from her purse, took one out and lit up.

"I can fix you something if you'd like. Dale could probably use some help with whatever he's doing out there," Mom said.

"Yeah."

"Or you could go see Jonny. Lord knows he isn't busy," she said.

I finished the coffee and put the mug in the sink, scratched my head and smoothed my hair. Truth was, I didn't want to see Jonny. Last time he brought me down. It wasn't just him being low. He was mean and arrogant. Acted like he knew it all.

It's hard to help a brother. Your own flesh and blood. He's too much like me, he's all the things I don't like in myself. I want to say he's on his own, it's his own battle. I have my battles too. I don't expect everyone else to fight them for me.

"I'll find some time soon. What're you thinking about fixing up for lunch?"

"I could make some ham sandwiches," mom said.

"Sounds alright," I said.

I was shaking from the coffee. Thoughts in my head like hornets. There was Mom, Becky, my job, the world, Jonny. He could make it a little easier on the rest of us. The way I look at it, the least we can do is not be a burden on others.

LEARNING TO LIVE

BALDY WILLIAMS GREW UP IN THE SUBURBS. He went to a private grade school, a private high school and a private university. His parents gave him an allowance and he worked as an assistant manager at a McChuckles family restaurant.

After he graduated from Wilmington he interned at Sackman and Brickby. After his internship he got a job at Turkelton. He carried a laminated card and wore collared shirts, nylon slacks and long stretchy socks. Two pairs of shiny black shoes that pinched his big toes. He sucked his dinners through plastic tubes from a company called tubefood.

Clumps of hair fell off his head. It was genetic. By his third year at Turkelton he was bald except for a few scattered wisps that glimmered in the sunlight. Baldy wasn't called Baldy until he lost his hair; as a child he was called Barry or William. The rest of his body looked as if it were collapsing in on itself; his stick arms stuck to his sides, his shoulders rolled forward, his head was small and round like a sucked lollipop. His nose narrow and his eyes like still puddles in a dirt path the day after a rain.

Baldy got promoted to auxiliary facilitator and then he shaved his head with a straight razor. He bought a kit from a company called Warwick's; it came with an aftershave lotion, scalp oil and towel. After shaving and rubbing in the oil his head shone more brilliantly than his shoes.

He was thirty and still had time to find a wife. Some of the women in his company looked good to him; they wore tight skirts and smelled like fruit. They used lewd language, especially when others could hear them. But they liked Jud Crulow. He was a senior coordinator of team building and development.

Jud lifted weights and wore suits from Portugal. He'd been divorced and saw his kids every other weekend. He had tanned skin, a white smile and lacquered black hair. Jud spread his arms and legs on the train. He massaged shoulders and slapped backs and laughed with his mouth wide open and his head rolled back. There were rumors about his relationships with some of the women at the company.

"We gotta loosen you up!" he'd say to Baldy.

Some days Jud would take Baldy aside and lean into him, lower his head a little and, with his eyes scanning the room, drop his voice and whisper something suggestive about a nearby woman. Baldy would laugh and say,

"Oh yeah, for sure."

Baldy had always listened to his parents. He studied, worked and saved money; he denied himself many pleasures. When Jud talked about his adventures, when he made comments about not getting enough sleep the night before and then winked, Baldy wondered what it was like.

One day Jud looked at Baldy and said "you know what you need to do?" He put his hand on Baldy's shoulder and shook it.

"Skydive."

"I don't know."

"I'm telling you, there's just about nothing more freeing than jumping out of a plane. You'll be a different man when you land."

***

Baldy bought a house in the shape of a cylinder. His house was the only one with that shape on his street and it was made of energy efficient materials. Construction workers put it up in a week. Baldy would come by and check on the house. Swarthy men caked with plaster and dust stared back at him in silence and went back to sawing and hammering. When the house was ready Baldy had another team of men move his furniture. He bought surveillance equipment that talked to him.

Baldy's house was narrow but it had five floors. He slept lightly in his temperature-controlled bed. His androgynous computer assistant woke him up every morning. He traveled to the bottom of his house in a cylindrical elevator which let out a whooshing sound as it moved up and down.

One weekend morning Baldy woke up in a dour mood. The sky was a dismal grey. He thought about Jud and supposed he was doing something adventurous or interesting, like bungee-jumping or cooking breakfast for a woman he'd met the night before. Baldy assumed Jud never woke up on a weekend morning and let a grey sky bring him down.

***

"How was your weekend?"

"Pretty low-key, really. Just took my bike a hundred miles up

I-sixty-six to Grizzly's Ridge. I woke up and I knew I had to get away."

"Haha, yeah. I've never been up to Grizzly's Ridge. I hear it's beautiful."

"Oh man, you have no idea. I know the perfect spot for catching the sun. It's really high up there."

Baldy told Jud of the time when he was six years old and rode a Ferris wheel at the county fair. They had to shut it down and let him off because he wouldn't stop crying. Baldy's dad screamed obscenities at the carney who pulled a big lever and the Ferris wheel made a harsh metallic sound; the families stuck at the top yelled with excitement.

"Poor guy," Jud said. "That's the problem right there, ya know? That experience scarred you."

"I never really liked amusement parks," Baldy said.

"Amusement parks are alright. You got nothing to worry about on those rides, ya know?"

"It's that feeling in my stomach…"

"I'm going to get you to skydive. You're going to jump out of a plane."

"You've done it before, right?" Baldy asked.

"Oh yeah, I do it at least once a year."

Baldy said he might do it and then excused himself for a meeting. Jud walked off saying he was going to set it all up; his voice echoed through the lobby.

***

"Today will be sunny and warm, with a high of eighty-four, light winds and clear skies," said the device.

"Thank you, Casey," said Baldy.

He couldn't believe he'd agreed to do it. He was skydiving with Jud. When he woke up that morning the atmosphere was alien. The world had a pale green sickly tint, like a show playing on an old television after a kid twiddles the knobs on the control panel.

Baldy trembled in the plane but tried to hold it in. Jud told stories about himself. He talked of his drug use and how he never got addicted. Baldy asked about the odds of a parachute failure.

The instructor with a small mustache and razor burns on his neck unlatched the door and slid it open.

"Okay guys, it's time to fly," he said as the air rushed in and whipped their clothes.

One man jumped. Then another. Now it was Baldy's turn. Jud grabbed his shoulders and shook them.

"You're going to be fine."

Baldy plummeted and felt reborn. He grabbed his cord and tugged on it. He heard a snapping sound and he saw the cord out in front of him. In a blink his body had fallen beneath it.

He might have described it as the most real and unreal moment of his life, the only thing that had happened and something that could not happen ever. He had time to think. His lifetime of control and obedience had come to nothing, swiftly and necessarily and yet without justification.

Baldy's cheeks flapped, the air blasted his gums. He slid out of his backpack and looked over it. There had to be a way to open the parachute without the cord. He fumbled over belts, straps, pouches and buttons. Why were there so many pockets and flaps? They'd gone over it on the ground. First Jud and then the instructor pointing to colored illustrations. Baldy read articles and pamphlets and had practiced pulling the cord.

He'd fallen for a long time and he could see green and brown patches below. Suburban streets and apartment complexes, power lines and cellphone towers. The backpack slipped out of his hands. Baldy wondered how the ground would feel. By now Jud had jumped and opened his parachute.

ANTECHINUS

THE SILVER DOOR HANDLE LOWERED WITH A CLANK. The door swung open and the doctor walked in holding a clipboard.

"You've tested positive," the doctor said.

He coughed.

Vincent had been sitting in the room for an hour by himself, his legs dangling from the pale green examination bed, his eyes wandering the white walls.

"Am I going to die?" Vincent asked.

"Excuse me. HRRRAAGH."

Silence except for the buzzing of fluorescent lights. Then the doctor said:

"Not necessarily. Not anytime soon. No, you could live a very long and healthy life. But it all depends on one thing. You can never have sexual intercourse with a woman."

"What?"

"If you have penetrative sex with a woman," the doctor stopped, took off his glasses and wiped them on his white coat and continued:

"If you so much as place the tip of your penis inside a vagina, you will die. In about an hour or two. But, if you don't ever have vaginal sex, then you can live as long as anyone else."

"I guess I can do that," said Vincent.

"I'm going to need to speak with your parents about this. Your mom is in the waiting room?"

"Yes."

"I'll have Cindy schedule a phone consultation, I have to see another patient here in forty-five seconds. I wish I had a packet to give you, a website to go to, a forum, something. But this thing is brand new. You're the first case. We'll come up with some educational material," said the doctor.

"Wow," said Vincent.

"It's a good thing we caught it when we did, before you became active."

***

The doctor explained it to Vincent's mom. She was on the phone in the garage.

"An hour after the tunica albuginea absorbs the vaginal mucous from the Bartholin's gland, Vincent's immune system will attack his organs. It will start with his liver and then move to his kidneys. Everything will shut down. The whole process will take an hour, two at the most. There could be vomiting of blood, defecating of blood. It won't be pretty."

"Oh my," she said.

"But there's nothing else wrong, he won't have any other problems?"

"Other than that, he's a perfectly healthy young man."

"And there's nothing he can take?"

"As of now, no, there's nothing. We're all banking on gene therapy. I'd say there's some hope. If we can figure out a way to edit that code, just snip out that problem sequence, then he'll be good as new. We have smart people working on it. Could be two years, could be ten years, could be thirty, hard to say. If they can fix this they can fix just about anything, so we'll all be pretty happy at that point," the doctor said.

He laughed like paper getting wadded up.

"Okay," she said.

Silence except for the hum of the second refrigerator.

"Is there anything else you'd like to know?" the doctor asked.

"Uhh, should we do anything to help prevent him from having sex? Can he masturbate?"

"I almost forgot to mention that. Yes, masturbation is just fine. It's healthy for everyone, good for a man's prostate. But in his case it will save his life. Hell, it's probably saved who knows how many lives.

Encourage him to masturbate as much as possible. The only thing you can do is dampen or redirect the urge. And, if it gets bad enough, there are other ways of doing that. Chemical castration is an extreme measure, but it's an option. We'd like to prescribe masturbation first, see if that keeps his desires in check. Plenty of porn should do the trick. Doesn't matter too much what he likes, as long as it keeps him away from real women."

That was the end of it. His mom stood in the cool garage that smelled of oil and rubber and plastic toys. She looked at the door and thought of how she would talk to her husband and son.

The door to the kitchen seemed to draw back until it was a speck of white against a black void. She took a few steps and then called the doctor's office again. It went to voicemail. After the piercing beep that sounded like the wrong answer in a game show, she drew in a breath as if to leave a message and then she hung up and called again.

The receptionist answered and transferred her call. Earth Wind and Fire played. A robot voice said thank you for holding. More funky bass and drums. She looked at the door to the kitchen and it had returned to its normal spot. The garage recovered its usual dimensions.

"Yes?"

It was the doctor. The long hold had lulled her.

"Oh, I have a few more questions."

"Go right ahead."

"Can he do other stuff? Like, anything oral or anal, or maybe with a man?"

A pause, then the sound of papers shuffling. A stapler clanking in the distance.

"Hmm, you know, it didn't occur to me. You have to remember this is all brand new. We've just never seen anything like this before. I don't see why not. I'd say all that's on the table. He can get handjobs, blowjobs, anal sex should be fine. Really he'd be much better off gay, if you can influence him that way. Much safer."

"I don't think he's gay. He's never said anything about liking boys."

"Well, you might want to make sure. He could be hiding it. Everyone's a little gay. It's a spectrum, you know. I'm personally pretty far down on the scale, not a lot of gay interests. Sometimes I wish things were otherwise, seems easier in some ways. But he probably has some natural curiosity. I'd encourage it, if possible. Maybe have him watch a movie with one of those heartthrobs, a Ryan Gosling type or something. I don't even know who the kids are into these days. Talk about how handsome the men are in a *Fast and Furious* movie. Have him read some classical Greek philosophy.

"Come to think of it, I will say, if he's doing some of the other stuff with women, it's a little risky. It might be tough for him to stop at the right time, put the brakes on. Speaking from experience."

"Okay. I don't know what to do," said the mom.

"I recommend therapy, counseling, a sex therapist, a cognitive behavioral therapist. There are many psychological treatment modalities. We could get him a specialist to help with his transition into a queer identity, if necessary. Might suggest an asexual identity, we're seeing more of that these days too. I'll have Cindy send some pamphlets with resources, directories, agencies, nonprofit organizations, hotlines. We don't know much about this condition, but there's a lot of support for various disorders and issues, plenty of overlap among them, we'll find something that'll help."

"Alright."

"You know, it's really not a bad time to have this condition. Society doesn't place as much value on heterosexual intercourse anymore. The procreative stuff isn't as important. Your son has plenty of options. He can still enjoy a rich sex life. Okay I have to go now, I have a patient right in front of me."

The phone clicked; a dreadful silence engulfed the garage. She walked to the door and opened it. No one in the kitchen. She walked into the living room and around the first floor of the house. Through the dining room window she saw her husband in the yard raking leaves under towering elms. She heard the rustling of the rake. Beyond the yard was a sidewalk and freshly paved blacktop. A row of neat houses and straight drives. Watching over the suburban panorama was a wistful autumn sky, stained with purple like spilled wine.

She called to Vincent.

***

He went to therapy. They tried to gauge his interest in boys. Tried to reassure him, tell him it was alright if he had those feelings. Everyone still loved him, wanted the best for him. If he was gay he could be open, he could express himself, explore his desires. The thought of kissing another boy made him dry heave.

All day at school he looked at girls. Their soft glowing skin, their shining eyes. Breasts that seemed to grow by the hour. The shapes of their legs, the way they walked. He listened to their laugh. Felt something deep within him, something that preceded him and had been waiting for him to embody it. A desire to touch and hold and consume these creatures, one after the next.

They moved and sparkled as if they came from a different planet. He was made of dirt and they were crafted with light and air. His head spun and floated in contemplation of them. It kept him awake at night. His erection trembled, it stood up and waved like a conductor's wand; his sheets stuck to his groin in the morning.

He went to high school where the girls were curvier and wore makeup and acted like they knew what they were doing, like they had already mastered this ancient practice and were on the inside of a world he could only see from a distance. Other boys talked about getting blowjobs and word got around about certain girls. Nothing could ever be confirmed.

At seventeen, Vincent had never touched a girl, other than hugging his mom and grandmothers and cousins on holidays. He had crushes, girls he dreamed about more often than others. Almost every girl interested him, but there was one who frequented his reveries.

Amelia in seventh period algebra. He'd catch her glancing at him. She had long black hair and dark flashing eyes. Her hips and breasts seemed ready to burst through her clothes. She wore short skirts. Sometimes she spread her legs a little under her desk and his soul rushed to fill the space. He wanted to fit between all her parts, fit inside her every opening, hide his whole being within her.

They walked down the halls together. Blinding white tiles under searing fluorescence. The clanging metal lockers, the torrent of talk. They chatted about the homework they didn't do, the miniseries they watched instead. She mentioned other boys. The name of another boy in her mouth scrambled his guts, set his skin on fire. He'd swallow like he was trying to choke down a cork.

No one told him how girls worked, what they liked. His parents and therapists and doctors reminded him every day that girls would kill him. It was fine to be their friend. Anything else could lead to a grisly death. His dad had no practical advice, never talked about his own experience. It was as if he'd been given a factory-issued wife and hadn't kept the instructions. All events and experiences came to everyone else. Other people got into the mix, could touch and rub the inside of life; he was behind glass.

They encouraged him to use porn. But he'd been watching it for years. He remembered his first clip. A woman on her knees, shot from the waist up, a giant veiny dick in her face. She sucked and jerked the jutting penis with a soulless look in her eyes. Vincent felt queasy and anxious like he'd pulled a fire alarm. Some obscure part of himself whispered that he'd broken a sacred order. Not only had he intruded upon what should've been a private act between two people, his own decency had been violated by the obscene exhibition.

His disgust mingled with arousal. He absorbed countless acts and scenarios, saw respectable roles turned into septic parodies. Blowjobs, threesomes, foursomes, cumshots, double penetration. Twisted limbs, tireless thrusting, operatic orgasms. The arousal overcame the disgust, boredom followed. Watching porn regressed from a blood pressure spiking event to a tepidly pleasurable routine, like the thousandth sweet soda dimly recalling those first few sugar rushes.

Amelia got a boyfriend. It was inevitable, like the southward flight of birds in the winter. His name was Adam, he played strong safety and took AP chemistry classes. Vincent stopped talking to Amelia and spent more time playing video games and watching funny clips on his phone. His parents would check in, ask if he'd been feeling tempted by girls.

"What about condoms? Would that protect him? Could he have sex with a woman if he wears a condom?" His mom asked the doctor over the phone.

"Well, it would lower the risk somewhat. But not by much. Condoms don't provide full coverage of the entire penis. We haven't figured out how to really vacuum seal that bastard on there. The problem is that if any vaginal secretion touches any part of the skin of his penis or scrotum, the deadly reaction will occur."

***

Vincent graduated high school and went to the state university an hour north of his hometown. Fifty-thousand students. He didn't have a major, didn't know why he went. Everyone said the experience was important, any degree would improve his job prospects, help him avoid menial labor, the service industry. His first semester he took courses in literature, sociology, finite mathematics, hapkido and the history of rock and roll.

One fall day between classes he saw Amelia walking down a wending brick path. Her figure shimmering and unreal against the postcard backdrop. Leaves had changed colors and lay about the trimmed grass and shaved stone. Malformed landscapers shoveled mulch and watered flowers like medieval peasants bound to the manor of a haughty lord.

Vincent's heart beat like a machine gun and his skin warmed as he walked to her. They hadn't talked in months. He didn't know she'd gone to the same school.

They ate a late lunch at the food court. Over pizza with grease pooling in the cheese, Amelia told Vincent what happened with her boyfriend.

"We planned to come here together. We were going to live in the same dorm. We even scheduled classes at the same time. I'm a physics major. He was doing biology for pre-med. The day before we moved into the dorms he broke up with me," she said.

"I'm sorry. Did he say why?"

"He didn't want to be tied down. A bunch of other stuff," she said.

Vincent took a big bite and a pepperoni slice slid off the pizza and hit his shirt. She went on.

"I thought we were in love. We both said I love you. He didn't act like he was interested in anyone else. I thought we were going to make it."

"Seems like most people break up when they go to college. I don't know what to say, probably nothing that will make you feel better. But that's how guys are, from what I hear. I guess I mean that's how people are," said Vincent.

"What's so important about having sex with random people? That's what they mean, when they say they want to be free, or alone, or independent, or whatever. It means they want to be with everyone. Why is that worth losing someone you love?"

"I don't know. I wouldn't know anything about that."

"I know you have a condition. I know it's different for you."

"It makes things easier in some ways. I don't have to worry about any of that," said Vincent.

"It's not that great. Sex, I mean. It is great, when you care about someone."

Vincent stared at what remained of his pizza, the cardboard crust. Students walked by their table, talking of classes, cool or lame professors, flings and upcoming parties. Hair-netted food court employees pressed burger patties down on scalding flattops, put pickles on hoagies. Some were students; others were much older men and women who hadn't gone to school.

"I just want to do it. I want to know what it's like. I try not to think about it. Seems like it just hurts people, anyway. Everyone's always getting heartbroken. They tell themselves it's all just fun. But if you just wait a little, something bad seems to happen at some point. Someone gets hurt. But it's weird to not go through it. Feels like I'm missing out."

"I only wanted Adam. I don't care about having sex. I only wanted to do it with him because we were together and I thought it meant something. It feels like he took something from me, something he doesn't even care about."

"Are you talking to anyone else? Have you met anyone you like?" Vincent said.

"No, I don't think about it. Nobody stands out like that. People blur together."

They met every day between classes. Walked in the cooling air as the leaves fell, sat on stone ledges and watched students stream out of brick buildings. In the evening he went to her dorm when her roommate was gone. They sat on the floor with their backs against her bed.

Vincent talked to his parents every few days. They asked how his classes were going, if he'd met any boys.

"I've been talking to your doctor. He hasn't heard anything new about gene therapy. But he did tell me they're getting much better at gender reassignment surgery. If that's something you might be interested in" his mom said.

"If I become a woman I can live a normal life," Vincent said.

"You can have a normal sex life."

Vincent was in his dorm, alone. The mini fridge whirred; he could hear someone playing video games in the next room over. *Aggravated Assault 3.*

"You know, if you want to be with a girl, you can have anal sex," his mom said.

"Mom, I don't like talking about this with you."

"There's nothing to be ashamed of. We should be able to

discuss these things. We just want you to be happy," she said.

"I think I'd be happier if I just didn't have to deal with it."

"Well, accidents can happen. You need to be careful."

"Accidents. Things just happen. That's what people say. Nothing just happens with me."

"You think too much, honey," his mom said.

The semester went on, color drained from the earth. Naked tree branches ranged out spindly and sharp against a plated sky like crudely fashioned surgical tools. Vincent hadn't made any friends his own age except Amelia, but every week he went to the office hours of his literature professor Doug. They were almost never interrupted by other students.

In a drab office overrun with half-skimmed books, the two men, separated by twenty-five years, talked as near equals. Vincent had a quiet seriousness that drew professorial types to him. Doug put his feet on his desk, he stroked his stubbled chin as Vincent filled him in on his condition.

"And you've never felt any inclination toward men? I suppose all your troubles could be avoided if you had homosexual leanings."

"I'm disgusted by men. All I've ever wanted is to know what it's like to be with a woman, what pussy feels like," said Vincent.

"I have to level with you. It's like nothing else."

Doug peered into a great depth, seemed to recall a treasure of erotic experiences. A dreamy look settled on his face for some time, then his features tightened.

"Well, it's not all magic and sunshine. I've had my fair share of romantic devastation. Sexual love opens us up to tremendous pain, betrayal that can't be reckoned with. What's so fascinating to me is that there's just no precedent for this. AIDS is the closest thing, but we've figured out how to contain that, treat it. It's basically not a problem anymore. For you, sex is a literal death sentence. Even in literature, there's pretty much no analogue," Doug said.

"I've never even kissed a girl. I don't know how to make moves, I don't know what the point is if I can't have sex," said Vincent.

"I get that. Women are very horny. They sometimes still act coy about these things, although not as much anymore. They really want to be fucked. You could be the sweetest guy, someone they really respect and look up to, but if you're not fucking them, you're like furniture or something, maybe a machine to get other things. They'll never really love you," said Doug.

"I know that. It's funny how I know that even though I've never experienced it. People tell you all kinds of bullshit about how it doesn't matter, you can still find love. But I know it's not true. It's like we're born with the knowledge of how things really work, what's really important, everything is set up to work a certain way, and it can only work that way. All the talk around it is just to make the freaks feel better," said Vincent.

Doug took his feet off his desk and sat up straight in his rolling chair. He seemed possessed by a profound idea.

"Yes, that's it. You do have an understanding that's unnatural for your age. Having a rare mind, or condition, it isolates, you can't relate to anyone, but you are compensated with insight. In a way, it's a gift. But it's incredibly lonely. All gifted minds struggle with this."

"I'm only special in a negative way. I'm not bright, I have no real talents. Even if I worked hard at something, distinguished myself somehow, this would always bring me down, cancel it all out," said Vincent.

"I understand that feeling. Still, I want you to know that I hope this doesn't get the best of you. There has to be a way to contribute something of value to the world. Idiots can fuck, they reproduce all the time, it's about all they can manage. Obviously it's important, we'd die off without that ability, but there have to be other things that make life worth living. Isaac Newton was reportedly a virgin. Gogol was rumored to have been impotent."

"Maybe when I invent a new form of math I'll feel a little better about myself."

"Of course this is all easy for me to say. I've fucked a lot. At the same time, I often wonder what it's all amounted to. I'm divorced, no kids. When I was younger I dreamed of writing a great work. That's nothing special, many of us dream of such things. Time has passed, I never got around to it. I've written critical articles, as you know. But no one reads those now, no one will even be able to find those when I'm dead. It will be buried in the great mass of scholarly output. So what has it all meant? But damn, some of the women I've been with..."

***

For days, a heavy gray sky portended snow. The air was electric. Finally, the snow fell. The semester was almost over, Christmas break on the horizon. Students looked forward to going home and hanging out with high school friends. They tried to focus on finals.

Campus was covered in thick shining snow. Everything seemed perfectly preserved yet fragile, as if touching a tree would shatter it. Vincent and Amelia were in Amelia's dorm after dark.

They should've been studying but they'd been talking for hours. They didn't drink so they talked about the flaws and insecurities of students who partied.

After midnight the conversation stalled. They sat next to each other and fidgeted. Looked into each other's eyes until the intensity overwhelmed them. Slight nervous smiles broke on their faces and then they looked away.

Gazing into nothing, Vincent asked:

"Can I kiss you?"

He knew it was the wrong thing to do. Far from the slick behavior of an experienced lover. The transition from talking to kissing should've been continuous, but he fumbled it and stitched those sequences together with extraneous dialogue like a bad editor. He couldn't do otherwise.

She said nothing for what seemed like weeks. She put her hand on his.

"Yes."

Her lips were soft and warm. He drifted on a current of bliss. It was as if the loneliness had never been, his entire past of longing and isolation bunched up into this moment and redeemed.

They kissed and stopped to look at each other, silent and vibrating with fulfillment, then kissed again, their tongues sliding tenderly, a wordless talking that said *how much I've wanted this*. It went on for an hour. Amelia took off her shirt, Vincent took off his. They moved to her bed.

Soon they were naked, their breaths short. Vincent's dick stood up straight against his belly. Her body was nothing like all those images. It was infinitely better, qualitatively of a different order. He knew then with visceral certainty what he had always suspected: the simulated act could never compensate him for the reality of a woman who desired his touch, who writhed and whimpered for him alone.

"Vincent, stop. We can't do this."

"I want to, please."

"It'll kill you. I can't."

"I don't want to live without it. I can't go on like this anymore."

"It's too much. I couldn't live with myself. It's not fair."

She moved away from him and sat up on the bed and bunched up her knees.

"I just can't. How could I bear that, knowing I was the reason you died?"

"I want to die. I want to do this with you."

"We don't even have a condom."

"That wouldn't help anyway."

"No, no, I can't. Think of your parents, your family. They'd think I was a murderer."

She grabbed the sheet and pulled it over her. Staring down at her knees, she said:

"I'm sorry, Vincent. I'm sorry you have to live with this. I can't help you, I wish I could. I want to be with you now, I'd be with you even if we can't do it. I don't care, it's not that important."

"Yes it is. We both know it is. I'd rather know what it's like, experience it with you than live another hundred years with the stupid fantasies. All those alternatives. It's no good."

He reached out and brushed her hair. Leaned forward to kiss her. She turned her head.

"Just wait a second. I don't trust myself right now. I'm sorry, Vincent. It's late, we're tired. You should go. We can talk about this later."

He got off the bed and put on his clothes, hoping she'd call him back. When his coat was on he stood and looked at her, waited.

"Okay, I guess I'll go."

Outside the dorm the frozen air flayed him. No one was around, nothing moved. All his life would be like this bare expanse, all light and dark surface, a dream of blood and heat. There was death in an hour of agony, and there was death in the slow stretch of days, which lay ahead like a mythic punishment.

He walked to his dorm, seeing no one on the way, and fell into bed, shivering with angst.